# A Graveyard of My Own

# A GRAVEYARD
# OF
# MY OWN

Ron Goulart

**Walker and Company**
**New York**

First published in the United States of America in 1985 by the Walker
Publishing Company, Inc.

Published simultaneously in Canada by John Wiley & Sons Canada,
Limited, Rexdale, Ontario.

**Library of Congress Cataloging in Publication Data**

Goulart, Ron, 1933–
 A graveyard of my own.

 I. Title.
PS3557.085G7  1985    813′.54    84-19678
ISBN: 0-8027-5605-0

Printed in the United States of America

Book Design by Teresa M. Carboni

10 9 8 7 6 5 4 3 2 1

*I believe I'll buy me a graveyard of my own,*
*I'm gonna kill everybody that have done me wrong.*

*—Trad. blues*

# Chapter One

*T*HE MORNING HE found the dead man had started off splen-
didly.

Warm sunlight came beaming into their big bedroom,
a rich assortment of cheerful birds commenced singing in
the budding branches of the trees outside the high, wide
windows.

Reluctantly, Bert Kurrie moved away from the slim,
auburn-haired young woman he'd been sleeping entangled
with. The digital clock on the rough-hewn bedside table
gave a small electronic jump, changing from 6:34 to 6:35.

"Time to be up and doing," muttered Bert, rising. He
was a long, lanky man of thirty-three.

Jan, mostly asleep, said, ". . . running?"

"If you're going to get the most out of it, you have to do
it every day." Resting one knee on the rumpled blue sheets,
he kissed her on her bare left shoulder.

Making a smiling sound into her pillow, she returned
to sleep.

Bert, clad in the candy-striped top of an ancient pair of
pajamas, wound his way around the cardboard cartons
piled up in the large rugless room. The damn things must
have mated and multiplied while he and Jan slept. He
knew he had unpacked dozens of them yesterday.

He went barefooting along the hardwood hallway and
into the upstairs bathroom.

A bathroom shared with a woman has an entirely different aura. This one, although only two days old, was already rich with the spicy sandalwood scent he associated with Jan.

But she didn't festoon it with frilly black undergarments the way Bert's first wife did. He took his running shorts and old sawed-off sweatshirt from the hook on the back of the door.

Whoa now with that first-wife stuff, he told himself. Let's concentrate on our present spouse and make no comparisons.

He and Jan had been married since the previous autumn.

Bert studied himself in the mirror over the sink. "Wow, how'd Errol Flynn get in there?"

He brushed his teeth and rinsed his mouth with a special organic mouthwash. Yawning, he struggled into his running attire.

Downstairs, perched atop one of the towers of unopened moving-van boxes, he found his old battered tennis shoes.

If you're going to keep up with this running mania, you'd better invest in the proper shoes, he thought. Otherwise, your fellow runners here in posh Fairfield County are going to give you the razzberry when you go zooming by.

Shoes dangling from his right hand, Bert wandered along another bare corridor. The living room was immense and, despite the warm spring morning pushing against the leaded windows, a bit chill. More boxes in here, all around the deep stone fireplace.

Maybe we don't ever have to unpack them, he reflected. We can pass them off as the latest thing in modular furniture.

He continued on to the back of the house and into the large studio which was one of the main reasons he and Jan had decided to splurge and rent this house in Brimstone, Connecticut. It had a terrific slanting skylight.

"Good morning." He'd noticed a surly-looking orange tomcat sitting, sphinxlike, up on a pane of the skylight. "Thought you guys were supposed to grin all the time."

The cat stared down at him for a few seconds before wrinkling his nose and gazing off elsewhere. He returned to scrutinizing the evergreens that rose high all around the studio.

Sitting down in his chair facing his drawing board, Bert tugged on his white-and-red socks and his threadbare tennis shoes.

He'd read someplace you could do permanent damage to your spine, as well as other important parts of your skeleton, if you went running without the proper shoes. He was easing into serious running gradually, though, and didn't feel quite ready to acquire the whole rig.

Bert realized, again, that he could now face the work he found on his board of a morning without flinching. He'd quit the comic-book business last year and surprisingly to him, though not to his wife, had been able to move into commercial art and illustration without any problems.

The sketch on the board was a rough for a paperback cover. It showed a very macho cowpoke slowly reaching for his six-gun and staring ominously out at the reader.

Okay, this won't get me an invitation to join the Royal Academy, he admitted to himself, but it's darn good. A hell of a lot more satisfying to do that the salivating lobster-men I was turning out for Maximus Comics, Inc.

The tomcat made a sly noise, went clicking across the skylight with his eye on a sparrow.

Bert tied his shoes, stretched up out of the chair, and trotted out of his brand-new studio.

Outside, the morning air was acceptable and invigorating. He'd found a four-mile circuit of back roads yesterday morning and figured to use it again today. The town of Brimstone was a good deal more rustic and foliage-laden than Westport, the nearby spot where he and Jan had been

*3*

living until they'd decided to make their move to larger quarters. A great leap forward, as his wife called it—aided in part by a small loan from Jan's father.

Their nearest neighbor was five acres away, protected from view by maples, oaks, and a New England stone fence. This part of town was crisscrossed with quiet tree-lined lanes, grassy meadows, and rocky hills. Ideal location for a solitary runner, especially if you didn't want too many people to notice you or discover that after about the second mile, you were usually wheezing like a canary bird.

He didn't realize he knew the corpse. Not at first.

Bert almost missed the body entirely. He was on his second mile, still breathing relatively normally. The narrow road dipped, twisting down alongside a rocky, nearly perpendicular hillside. At the foot of the two-hundred-foot drop was a scatter of large boulders and smaller, more jagged rocks. They filled an indentation off the road, a location they shared with brush and weeds.

As Bert came jogging downhill by the spot, arms and legs pumping evenly, a tiny chipmunk went scurrying across his path. It darted out of the woodlands on his right and into the rocks on his left.

Slowing, his glance automatically following the russet creature, he saw a leg and a white shoe.

What the hell . . . ?

He stopped, caught his breath, went over to investigate.

The dead man, clad in a maroon running suit, was on his back in among the big rocks, sprawled the same way someone who'd had a chair pulled out from under him would slump. Except his arms and legs were bent in wrong ways and his head was ruined, cracked and leaking blood and something else.

"Jesus," said Bert. "Jesus."

He gazed up at the hillside. There was a gap in the brush

4

up at the top. Yeah, and this poor bastard was still clutching a chunk of scrub in his bloody hand.

Flashlight over there, Bert noticed.

The lens was cracked in an ugly jigsaw pattern, although the bulb was still faintly glowing.

Make a good flashlight commercial. I fell to my death, but my Delco batteries kept right on burning.

Bert shook his head, hoping to clear it of the macabre jokes that the shock of seeing the smashed runner had set in motion in his mind.

Guy was obviously out running, one of these run-after-dark fanatics, he said to himself. Yes, hence the flashlight. He tripped up there in the dark, or maybe was sideswiped by a car. He falls, tries to catch onto the bushes, but it doesn't save him. Dumb to run after sundown in this sort of countryside, with no streetlights or . . . Holy Christ! It's Beau Jassminsky.

He'd been avoiding too close a look at the broken and bloody face. Now, almost by accident, he had stared into it and recognized a fellow artist.

Well, not much of an artist, actually. Jassminsky was an instructor at the Artist's Workshop, that overpriced correspondence school in nearby Westport. Nobody with any real ability would spend his days grading lessons from acned schoolboys and little old ladies in print dresses.

Bert had encountered Jassminsky at a few of the local artists and cartoonists' social gatherings. Sure, last month he and Jan had met the guy at a cocktail party over in New Canaan. Big jovial guy of forty or so. He'd patted Jan on the backside a few too many times. A gung-ho runner whom Bert had seen at one of the local minimarathons. Bert went to watch, not feeling quite ready yet to participate. Yeah, Jassminsky, all decked out in the latest running gear, had placed second in his division and had gone away with an immense gilded trophy.

Starting to frown, Bert took a step back from the dead man. What's wrong with this picture? he thought.

Yep, there was something not quite right.

He backed up a few more yards, like a painter sizing up his subject.

The shoes.

Head slightly tucked in, he approached Jassminsky's body again to make certain.

He's wearing tennis shoes, he confirmed. Almost as tacky as mine.

Jassminsky was the sort of runner who'd wear nothing but the best imported running shoes. He'd kidded Bert at that party when Bert mentioned he still ran in tennis shoes.

Beau would never go out for a run wearing these shoes.

So maybe he wasn't running when he fell.

Oh, so? Then why the warm-up suit, the headband, the light?

Hell, there had to be a simple explanation. This was nothing more than an accident. Go phone the police and then forget it.

It was an accident, that's all.

But it wasn't.

# Chapter Two

"*T*HEY LAUGHED?"

"Not too appropriate under the circumstances, but they did, yes."

Jan, dressed in pale-blue jeans and a checkered shirt, was sitting atop a large carton that had *kitchen* marked across its side in Bert's distinctive lettering. "You're a perceptive person, after all."

"A perceptive commercial artist, maybe, but not exactly on a par with Charlie Chan," he remarked, taking a sip of his freshly brewed peppermint tea.

"Did they imply you were merely a nitwit civilian and to keep your nose out of it?"

"Such was the impression I gathered from Detective Furtado and the uniformed guys."

She left her perch, hands fisting. "Well, I have faith in you and your perceptions." She crossed to the sink.

"Probably they're right and the business with the shoes means not a damn thing."

"No, you're right about Beau Jassminsky. He was the kind of dedicated jock who had to have exactly the right kind of fashionable equipment." She reached for the cold-water tap. "He wouldn't—you'll pardon the expression—have been found dead in the wrong sort of footwear. When he ran, he ran from head to foot. Our water's purplish, have you noticed?"

"Old pipes, haven't been used for a while."

"Did you make your tea with this purple water?"

"Boiling kills everything."

"You're more than likely guzzling down some fatal chemical waste right now. We best switch to bottled water."

Bert set aside his mug. "I'll try to forget the whole damn business. I'm a commercial artist, not a private detective."

"You're a good artist, though, meaning you've got a good eye." She turned the water off. "What exactly did the cops say?"

"To me, not much. 'Thanks for reporting this, Mr. Kurrie.' 'Stand back out of the way.' Dialogue like that."

"I mean about what killed Beau Jassminsky."

"A fall."

"An accidental fall?"

"Yep, completely and totally accidental," he said. "Even though, you know, he was wearing the wrong kind of shoes, it doesn't mean he didn't simply stumble in the dark."

"He ran that route every night for months."

"Did he?"

"Don't you remember his bragging about it at that party? He mentioned the fact between his attempts to leave a permanent set of his palmprints on my rear. Every night, he boasted, come rain or come shine."

"Okay, but for some reason he didn't see that rock."

"Which rock?"

"Police figure he tripped on a rock, fell and went tumbling over the edge." Bert decided to give the tea another try. "Jassminsky clutched at some brush on the way down."

"He was carrying a flashlight, you said. Why didn't he notice this rock?"

"Sometimes night runners just carry the light in their hand so people in cars will notice them, not to illuminate the roadways." He shrugged.

"What about footprints?"

"Ground up there is hard and dry, lots of gravel. Doesn't show much in the way of prints of any sort."

"I suppose it could've been just an accident," said Jan. "When you were late coming back and then you phoned . . . I thought maybe you'd had an accident yourself. Joggers are always falling down and breaking something."

"That's not actually true, Jan, more people fall down in bathtubs."

"Well, I am proud of you," she said, smiling. "You've taken up running. You've gotten back into illustration and you're doing terrifically. All darn commendable."

"It took the love of a good woman."

She laughed and put her arms around him. "Our new house is quite nifty, too. I'm glad we figured out a way to afford—"

The phone on the wall beside the sink was ringing.

"Might be a client." Bert eased free of his wife. "Hello?"

"Berton Kurrie, please."

"Speaking."

"Didn't get a chance to talk to you at the scene this morning, Berton. Mind if I call you Berton?"

"Yes, considerably. Use Bert. First, however, tell me who you are."

"Oh, Dick Weinberg, with the Brimstone *News-Pilot*," answered the boyish-sounding young man. "I'm covering the Beau Jassminsky death."

Clamping his hand over the mouthpiece, he said to Jan, "The press."

She went back to sit on an unopened carton.

"You found the body, is that correct?" asked Weinberg.

"Yes, that's it," he replied and gave him an account of his discovery of the remains.

"You yourself run that route every morning?"

"Intend to, we only moved into the area couple days ago."

"Oh, that's right. You're newcomers. And you're the one-time comic-book artist who—"

"I'd appreciate it if you didn't mention that in your story."

"Which? About your being newcomers or about your being a former comic-book great?"

"The comic book business."

"Okay, Bert," said the young reporter. "Now here's what I'm really curious about. You were arguing with Detective Furtado about something. The victim's shoes or something."

"Sort of arguing."

"What do the shoes have to do with your theory of the death?"

"Hey, I don't have any theory. By chance, I happened to be the first to notice the body. That's all."

"But what is it about his shoes?"

"They're not running shoes."

There was a silence. "That's it?"

"Yep."

"Not much."

"Nothing, probably."

"Well, thank you for your time, Bert. How do I, by the way, describe your profession? Cartoonist or artist or—"

"Commercial artist'll do. I've retired from the world of comics and cartooning."

"Okay, thanks again. Maybe I can do a profile on you for our feature section one of these days. I hear you're a fair artist."

"That I am. Bye." Bert hung up. "He didn't think much of the shoe angle, either. Guess I'll work at forgetting the whole mess."

"You can't do that."

"Sure, if I concentrate I can. I can probably induce a mild spell of amnesia if I . . ." He trailed off, shaking his head. "It was pretty grim, Jan. The way he looked, all smashed up like that. Hell, I didn't much like the guy, and he was a second-rate artist, but . . . you should've seen the way the cops took it in. Beau could've been a raccoon hit by a car. Just one more thing they had to clean up."

"They're in a different business than you."

"I better get back to the old drawing board or I may end up applying for Beau's job at the mail-order school."

Rising, Jan began peeling the tape off the carton she'd been sitting on. "I plan to devote the afternoon to unpacking."

"Yeah, I can help out soon as I finish up the rough I—"

The phone cut in again.

Jan suggested, "Must be the *New York Times* this time."

Bert answered. "Hello."

"Hey, I got it."

"Fortunately there's a cure. The process is painful, but—"

"I am alluding, amigo, to the job you recommended me for," said Juan Texaco.

"That's great."

"Only pays four hundred dollars per week, but it's just two days a week work," continued Texaco. "It'll help put me one step closer to escaping from the clutches of Maximus Comics, Inc."

"When Ty Banner told me he was looking for a new assistant on his *Dr. Judge's Family* strip, I figured you were a natural for the job."

"Especially when he listed the qualifications and 'brilliant' was the first item."

"Right, brilliant followed by 'works cheap.' "

"That's the tradition of my people, that's why we left the sun-drenched environs of Puerto Rico to journey to the bleak North. So we could work cheap for you Yankees," said his cartoonist friend. "Did it ever occur to you how much Banner's wife resembles Martha O'Driscoll?"

"Who?"

"A glamorous blonde who graced the screen in the by-gone 1940s."

"Can't place her."

"She looked just like Mrs. Banner."

"Ah, that Martha O'Driscoll."

"Before I journey back to my spartan digs in the Apple via a sleek Metro-North train, Ty is taking me to lunch in a Westport bistro known as the Inkwell Restaurant. We thought, as matchmaker, you might like to join in the celebration."

"Not exactly sure, Texaco."

"Are you too busy settling into your new and spacious digs to get away? Embroiled in creating yet another masterpiece of a paperback cover for—"

"Neither of the above."

"I just now noticed, old chum, that you sound a bit forlorn. Domestic trouble? No, that's impossible."

"Domestically, things are fine," answered Bert. "I'm sort of low because . . . well, I found a corpse this morning."

"A corpse? Where?"

"While I was out running. I guess I will join you guys. I'll tell you the details then."

"Anybody I know?"

"Don't think so, but Ty knows him. Artist named Beau Jassminsky."

"Not a murder or anything sinister, was it?" asked his friend.

Bert hesitated several seconds before replying, "No, just an accident."

# Chapter Three

THE INKWELL RESTAURANT sat on the edge of the Saugatuck River, about a block from the Westport train station.
As the framed drawings and photos on the walls testified,
it was a favored hangout of artists, cartoonists, and writ-
ers—free-lance people who didn't have to be much occupied with commuting schedules, neckties, and watercoolers.

Making his way through the crowded dining room, Bert
exchanged greetings with assorted friends and associates.
He spotted Texaco and Ty Banner at a table near one of
the restaurant's wide-view windows.

Banner was a handsome, though somewhat weathered,
man in his late fifties. Making a welcoming gesture with
the hand that held his martini, Banner said, "Hear you've
been out stumbling over cadavers, my boy."

Bert took a chair. Some kind of barge was chuffing by
out on the river. "I just happened to find Beau Jassminsky's body. It wasn't intentional."

The small, curly-haired Texaco inquired, "How's the
missus?"

"Splendid."

"Imagine living with a lass who's the spitting image of
Gene Tierney at her peak," sighed Texaco. "Few of us are
so fortun—"

"Jan doesn't look anything like Gene Tierney," Bert told
him. "She doesn't even have buck teeth."

"You're thinking of Bugs Bunny. Gene Tierney had merely a provocative overbite, which—"

"Care to fill us in on the accident?" Banner rested his elbows on the checkered tablecloth. "I used to know Beau pretty well. That was years ago, when we worked side by side in the funny-book business. I still used to see him around town now and then."

Texaco inquired, "You were in the comic-book biz, Ty?"

Bert caught the attention of a waitress and ordered a Perrier. "That was where, up at DC?"

"Nope, I never cracked the biggies. This was at Komic Kreations, Inc., which wasn't rolling in loot then as it is these days. We shared a loft down on Fourth Avenue in Manhattan with a brood of rats who were all in better condition than we were," answered the cartoonist. "That was long before KK got filthy rich off Captain Thunderbolt."

"Don't tell me, sahib, that I'm working part-time for one of the fellows who drew Captain Thunderbolt, World's Most Marvelous Man?" asked Texaco.

"No, I specialized in true crime, particularly true crimes committed by young wenches with immense knockers and fancy garters," replied Banner. "I was never a longjohn man, but I was in the shop there when poor Mack Gruber first came in with Captain Thunderbolt. Little did any of us realize that idiotic feature would save KK's bacon and make the owners bloody millionaires."

"It sure didn't make Gruber a millionaire," said Bert.

Banner nodded. "They really screwed the guy, the Komic Kreations folks. Got him to sign away all rights to his superhero. Nobody figured, except poor Mack, that a moronic strip like that would capture the fancy of the American public and found a whole empire. Not me, anyway. But then, I was also the lad who figured the Beatles would fade after about six months."

"You knew Gruber, huh?" Texaco scratched at his tight-curling hair. "I'm always fascinated with brother cartoonists who go completely goofy, since I'm planning to do that myself in my declining years."

"Sure, we were buddies." Banner straightened up. "Matter of fact, I saw Mack last week."

"In the loony bin?"

"No, no, right here in Westport. In front of Oscar's Deli. He's out."

"Climbed over the wall?"

"Mack was released some two or three months ago." Banner watched a seagull come swooping down to snatch something from the river. "He looked damned good; no trace of his breakdown shows. He always was a big, jocky sort of guy. Still is. Big, tanned, fit. Looks the way I ought to."

Bert tasted his Perrier. "Why's Gruber in Westport?"

"Mack's got a rich sister who resides in a palatial mansion down on the Sound. Millionaire's Row. Or is that, what with Reaganomics, Billionaire's Row now?"

"Whatever it is, it's a few steps up from Skid Row," observed Texaco, "which is where most old cartoonists end up."

"Nonsense, my boy," Banner said. "You have nothing to fear when it comes to your future. Since you're working for me, your old age will be comfortable."

"And not that far off," added Bert. "Working for Ty, you'll age forty years in six months."

"I'm a genial taskmaster," said Banner. "As well as a prince of good fellows."

"Well, you aren't as tough to work for as Carlotsky," admitted Bert, alluding to the managing editor of Maximus Comics, Inc.

"Can we return to Beau Jassminsky," suggested Banner. "This was an accident pure and simple, was it not? The minions of the law don't suspect foul play?"

Bert drank more of his sparkling water. "Sure, it was

*15*

an accident. Beau fell off a hillside while out running last night, dropped a couple hundred feet, and got pretty badly smashed up."

"I sense, my boy, you are not completely convinced it was accidental."

"The police are."

Texaco was gazing across the room. "Say, there's a young lady who has got to be an exact double for Dolores Del Rio in her prime," he said. "Imagine what neat offspring two gorgeous Latinos such as we could produce."

Banner persisted. "Do you suspect something, Bert?"

"No, I don't suspect a damn thing," he replied. "I am just going to keep at my drawing and let the Brimstone lawmen worry about why Beau Jassminsky was out running last night with the wrong shoes."

Blinking, Texaco asked, "Wrong shoes?"

"He was a fanatic jock," explained Bert. "The kind of runner who has to have everything that goes with the sport. He couldn't just read Jim Fixx's book and then go trotting around in old clothes. He had to patronize the best sports shops, load up on the latest kind of running clothes, shoes, headbands and so on. I saw him run in a ten-kilometer race once, and we talked to him at a party a few weeks back. He simply wasn't the kind of guy who'd go running in tennis shoes."

"He ran at night usually, didn't he?" said Banner. "So nobody was going to see him."

"That's not the point. Running, for guys like him, is almost a religion. You don't wear a hat in church, you don't run in tennis shoes."

"Can we expect," put in Texaco, "that you'll start wearing a costume, too, now that you're into jogging?"

"Running," he corrected. "Naw, I just do it for fun. Although I have been thinking about a pair of Adidas running shoes I noticed in a window on Main Street."

"You're already around the bend," said the little cartoonist, "if you're thinking about shoes instead of ladies."

"Besides this shoe clue," said Banner, "is there . . . huh, shoe clue. Try saying that ten times fast. But seriously, my boy, is there anything else that struck you as odd?"

"Not really, I guess."

"What do you think the business with the shoes means?"

"I mentioned it to the police. They think it means absolutely nothing."

"I want to hear your opinion."

"Well, it seems to me there are one or two possible explanations," Bert said slowly. "Could be Beau wasn't out running at all, but was up to something else. Or—and this is, I admit, damn farfetched—somebody else dressed him. Somebody who didn't know anything about running."

"Does sound unlikely," said Banner. "Why would somebody else dress the guy?"

"If he wasn't in any condition to dress himself."

"Dead already?"

"Or out cold."

A frown touched Banner's handsome forehead. "The police will be able to tell if Beau was drugged or conked before the fall."

"Sure. Except that fall messed him up pretty good. It might hide a blow on the head. I don't know."

Texaco was fidgeting. "This is getting too spooky," he complained. "I don't like the notion that a fellow artist was tossed over a cliff. It might start a fad, and I'm going to be working in the vicinity two days a week from now on."

"Okay, we'll shift gears," said Bert. "We'll talk about your new occupation."

"I want to thank you again," said Banner, "for bringing this little rascal to my attention. He's damn good, exactly what I was looking for to help out on the momentous chore of getting out six *Dr. Judge's Family* dailies and a Sunday page each and every week. He also looks like the sort who'll make a dandy caddy when I return to my neglected career as an ace golfer."

Texaco rose slightly in his chair, staring out the window. "Why would Carole Landis's double be going by in a sailboat?"

Banner turned to Bert. "Why does the chap keep seeing long-gone movie queens?"

"It's a rare genetic defect," explained Bert. "His father used to be an usher in a movie palace."

Banner finished his drink. "How goes domestic life?"

"It's all in boxes so far."

"If you ever have any problems, let me suggest a solution, old buddy."

"We don't have any problems. We haven't been married long enough for that. What makes you think Jan and I—"

"If, my boy, if," said Banner quickly. "I don't believe I've confided this bit of personal lore as yet, but I have joined a rap group, to expand my consciousness."

"Do people still do that?" Texaco ceased watching the blonde girl on the passing boat. "I thought rap groups went out with draft-card burning and blowing up college buildings."

"This one is for us more mature citizens," answered Banner. "Run by a guidance center here in Westport. We meet one night each week at different houses. All guys. We talk over our various problems, anxieties, hang-ups and aspirations."

"How many in your klatch?" asked Bert.

"Between six and ten. Even have a couple fellow artists in my cell. It's really been helpful to me, being able to get stuff out in the open. The past few sessions the topic's been guilt, and some quite interesting dirty laundry has been displayed. Here I've been brooding all my life about borrowing two bits from my Aunt Marie's purse when I was fourteen, while there are guys who've been carrying around burdens of guilt that dwarf . . . Ah, but we're not supposed to blab about what's discussed. That's part of the deal. An implied vow of secrecy."

"Sounds like about as much fun," said Bert, "as a meeting of the Cub Scouts."

"Scoff now, young fella, but when you reach your golden years, you may wish you had a rap group like mine."

"I've always considered lunches here at the Inkwell served that purpose."

"Nope, too undisciplined."

Texaco was frowning. "Bert, my people are noted for having second sight," he said. "All this talk about problems and guilt has given me the feeling you're in for more trouble."

Grinning, Bert asked, "Any specifics?"

"I think it has something to do with the death of Beau Jassminsky," his friend told him. "That business is maybe not over for you."

# Chapter Four

$B$ERT WAS DOING fine, all things considered.

It was an impressive Sunday morning, clear and warm. He wasn't as far back in the pack as he'd anticipated. Not that he was going to take home any trophies.

But, considering this was the first race he'd ever entered, he was making a good showing. Some three hundred runners had entered this ten-kilometer Westport fun run, and now, a shade over halfway into the race, Bert estimated he was in roughly 150th place.

A respectable showing. When he came flashing across the finish line, Jan, who was waiting back at Jessup Green, ought not to be too chagrined. He'd been worried, when on a sudden impulse he'd persuaded his wife to come into Westport with him this morning so he could sign up and run, that he'd finish in last place. Come in red-faced and wheezing, trailing behind an eleven-year-old schoolgirl and some senior citizen with a wooden leg.

But that looked as though it wouldn't be the case.

His lungs felt to be in excellent working order, there wasn't even a trace of a stitch in either of his sides. The new Adidas shoes he'd purchased yesterday, obviously in anticipation of entering this very race, fit perfectly and did seem to enliven his running in a way the old tennis shoes hadn't.

An image of Beau Jassminsky, dead and broken at the bottom of the cliff, popped into his head.

Bert tried to concentrate on the race. They were running along a quiet residential street now, a string of runners of varying age, sex, and shape. Substantial homes hereabouts, a few even stately—on two acres or more, with lots of sturdy trees, green lawns, prestigious automobiles.

A good many of the women entered in the race had long since passed him. No reason to be chauvinistic. Finishing around 150th wasn't exactly disgraceful.

After all, he'd never run this far before. Ten kilometers was just over 6.2 miles. He'd figured that out with the aid of the table in the back of his dictionary and his pocket calculator.

"You're Bert Kurrie, aren't you?"

Glancing to his right, he saw a pretty blonde young woman had caught up and was running beside him. Her hair was tied back with a black ribbon, her running shorts were scarlet and her T-shirt commemorated a past race. She wasn't wearing a bra.

"I am, yes," he replied, disappointed to find his voice had a dry, slightly wheezy quality.

"I'm Carolyn Frame." Her voice was natural and she had no trouble keeping pace with him. "I've seen your picture."

"They ran some in Maximus Comics back when I was—"

"No, in the files of our paper. I work for the Westport *Daily*," Carolyn explained. "I'm in want ads at the moment, although I want to move into investigative reporting. I'm a friend of Dick Weinberg."

"Do I know him?"

"He's with the Brimstone *News-Pilot*. He interviewed you about Beau Jassminsky's death."

"Yeah, that's right." He was finding it difficult to keep up small talk while running. Perhaps the more you did it, the easier it got.

"Dick told me you don't think it was an accident."

"He misquoted," said Bert, sucking in air. "All I mentioned was Beau wasn't wearing the right kind of shoes. Nothing very important."

"Dick is basically a sedentary type, a lardbutt really. So he doesn't know a thing about running," the blonde girl said. "The thing about the shoes didn't hit him as unusual."

"You think otherwise?"

They were running uphill now. Bert had to strain to keep up the pace. Over on his left, an eleven-year-old schoolgirl went whizzing by.

Carolyn wiped a trace of perspiration off her upper lip with the back of her hand. "I don't believe Beau Jassminsky's death was an accident at all."

Bert concentrated on cresting the hill. After he accomplished that, he asked, "What, then?"

"I'm pretty sure he was murdered."

He stumbled. "Murdered?"

"Right," she said. "And I think this murder was the second of what may be a series."

"Two hundred seventh isn't bad," Jan tried to assure him, "in a field of 326."

"I trailed a woman of mature years who was a grandmother. She finished 206th."

"So? It was your first race, after all."

"Hers, too." He dug in the sand with his big toe.

They'd driven down to the Sound and were sitting on a thin stretch of relatively empty beach. The afternoon was turning chill; a breeze was drifting in across the water.

"Well," said Jan, watching a white yacht that was sailing by, "next time maybe you won't be so distracted by sexy blondes in skimpy shorts and you'll be able to concentrate more on your running."

"Carolyn Frame's a reporter," he said. "I already explained that to you."

His wife picked up a handful of sand, then let it flow slowly out of her hand. "Working in the want-ad department doesn't make you a reporter."

"Maybe so, but she's a lot brighter than that lunk from the *News-Pilot.*"

"Prettier, too."

"She understood, being a runner herself, what my notion about Beau's shoes was all about."

"They're burying him day after tomorrow," said Jan, flinging the last of the sand into the wind. "Which seems to mean the police are satisfied that the poor man just fell."

"No, there's more to this than that. Especially if Beau's death is maybe number two in a series of—"

"Nobody thinks that except this dippy blonde. She's so anxious to get a scoop, she'd make up a story to—"

"Carolyn Frame might be wrong," he said. "Thing is, Jan, I want to find out what really is going on."

"Why?"

"Well, for one thing, I found his body," he answered. "That makes me feel involved."

"Suppose this gorgeous blonde hadn't approached you, would you still feel like that?"

Bert considered the question. "Yep, I would," he answered finally. "There really is some kind of puzzle here, and the damn thing keeps nagging at me. Something is wrong about Beau Jassminsky's death, and I want to find out what."

"And you'd like to show the police—Detective Furtado and the rest—that they're wrong?"

He nodded. "Probably so," he admitted. "Yeah, that is part of it. They're laughing at me, treating me like a rube."

"You're going to see her tonight?"

"We are. I told her we'd drop over about nine. She has a place over in New Canaan near—"

"I intend to devote this evening to uncrating the contents of our spacious living room," Jan said. "You can tackle her on your own."

"You trust me to visit her alone?"

"Of course."

He started to put his socks back on. "I don't know if that's a compliment or not."

# Chapter Five

*F*IREFLIES FLICKERED IN the darkness surrounding the shingle cottage, crickets serenaded. A single bat came gliding out of the weeping willow near the curving flagstone path.

Automatically, Bert ducked. "Atmosphere," he muttered as he straightened up.

By the time he got to the front door, it had been opened. Carolyn Frame stood in the rectangle of light. "You need a new muffler," she said.

"It is a new one."

"You got taken then. C'mon in." She was wearing a denim skirt and a candy stripe shirt, no shoes or stockings. Her blonde hair was still damp from a shower. "Wife couldn't make it?"

"We just moved into a new house and she—"

"Beer?"

Her living room was small, thick with old-fashioned furniture. Bookcases crowded with a jumble of paperbacks, hardcovers, magazines, and rag dolls covered two of the walls. A big stone fireplace gaped empty; an undressed Raggedy Ann sprawled across the left andiron. All of the tables and most of the chairs had rag dolls lolling on them, singly and in bunches.

"I don't drink anymore," he said, stopping beside a bentwood rocker that housed a golliwog that had lost most of its stuffing. "A Perrier'll be okay."

"Too expensive. Settle for club soda?"

"Sure."

"Go ahead and sit. You can move the doll. I collect them."

"So I surmised." Gingerly he placed the doll on the rug, clear of the rocker. "How long've you been with the West-port paper?"

"A year next month." Carolyn moved toward the kitchen. "I should've been a reporter by now. My mistake was doing too good a job in want ads."

"I had the same problem when I worked for Maximus Comics, Inc. They . . ." She'd left the room.

"Keep talking. I can hear you."

"Well, I was pretty good at drawing comics and they kept raising my page rates. That set up the temptation to stay there longer than—"

"Damn!"

"Something?" He left the chair.

The young woman came out of the kitchen with her forefinger pressed to her lips. "I keep cutting myself with the damn opener," she explained.

"We can skip the drink," he suggested, "and get right down to the subject of Beau—"

"No, I believe you have to finish each job you start." Smiling, she returned to the kitchen.

"Did you know Beau Jassminsky?"

"Damn."

"Another cut?"

"I just spilled some beer on my skirt."

"Could I maybe lend a—"

"No need." Carolyn returned carrying a tray that held two paper cups and a plate with taco chips on it. Elbowing a stuffed giraffe and two elves off the coffee table, she set the tray down. "Not only don't I have a decent set of real glasses, my paper cups don't even match."

Bert took the cup of sparkling water. "Cheers."

"What were you asking me?"

"About knowing Beau."

"I didn't know him, no." She took the other cup, settled on the arm of the narrow green sofa. A row of slumped rag dolls occupied all the cushions. "But I know someone who did."

He watched her as she sipped her beer. "Someone who thinks Beau was murdered?"

"Look, I'm going to get around to asking you to do a favor for me," she said. "I guess I have a somewhat ambivalent attitude toward all this. For one thing, I think there may be a hell of a newspaper story here. But . . . well, I'm also very worried about someone I'm fond of."

Nodding, Bert said nothing.

The young woman set her cup on the floor. "Do you know Dolph Tunney?"

"Not too well. He runs that art-supply store in Westport, but I find his prices are much higher than—"

"I'm involved with Dolph."

"Okay."

"What I mean is, he's married and all that. Older than me, too." She spread her hands wide, shrugging. "I like him a lot. Even though we can't see each other as regularly as we'd like." She shrugged again. "Amazing, isn't it, how many people's lives are like second-rate soap opera? I wouldn't even be confiding any of this in you. Except I have a feeling you can help."

"Help how?"

"I think . . . I'm not certain, but I've got a hell of a strong suspicion . . . that Dolph knows something about Jassminsky's death. About what really happened."

"Knows because he was involved in Beau's death?"

"No, he had nothing to do with that." Her long blonde hair brushed at her shoulders as she shook her head. "It isn't that at all." Reaching out, Carolyn picked up the nearest rag doll. It was a forlorn creature, a red-haired girl made of old sox. "I rescued most of them from the Goodwill and thrift shops."

"How exactly is Dolph Tunney involved, then?"

"Maybe I'm seeing a plot where there isn't one." She tugged absently at the doll's lumpy left leg. "I'll tell you, Bert, I entered that race hoping you'd be in it, so I could get a look at you. I watched you for a couple of miles and decided you look like a decent, sensible man."

"Yep, that's always been one of my handicaps."

"I decided it was okay to talk to you," Carolyn told him. "Here's what got me to worrying. I was having lunch with Dolph, in one of the out-of-the-way places we use, the day you found Beau Jassminsky's body. The story had come into the *Daily* and I mentioned it to Dolph, since I was fairly sure he knew Jassminsky."

"And he did?"

"Oh, yes," she replied, twisting the doll's leg. "When I told him . . . he looked very upset for a minute, maybe even frightened. He said, mostly to himself, 'That's two of us down.' Then he added, 'Somebody's got a little list, but where'd they get it?' "

"You obviously asked what the hell he was talking about?"

"When I tried to get Dolph to explain, he pretended it was nothing. He was naturally shocked to hear of an old friend's accidental death and he just blurted out some nonsense." She dropped the woebegone doll back on the sofa. "He was lying to me, I'm sure."

"He apparently thinks somebody besides Jassminsky was killed recently," he said. "Any idea who?"

"None, and Dolph won't talk about the subject anymore at all."

"Which brings us to a dead end."

"No, not really." She stood. "If you'd talk to Dolph, tell him how you discovered the body and that you're absolutely certain he was killed by someone . . . well, that might convince him to tell us what he knows. And really make him realize he's possibly in danger himself."

"He probably already knows that."

"It could be it's easier for him to believe that this was just an accident," she said. "Besides, I want to know what the hell this is all about. I . . . I'm in love with Dolph. It's stupid, but I am anyway."

"Then you ought to be able to get him to tell you what's going on."

"I can't, though." She walked over to the dead fireplace. "I'm supposed to meet him tomorrow night."

"Where?"

"His place. Dolph's wife and children—two boys, eleven and sixteen—are going away tomorrow to spend a week up at the Cape with relatives. When she's away, I . . . see him there, at his home."

"You want me to come along?"

"Exactly. I think it'll work. Get him to open up."

"You know, if I were him, I wouldn't want me tagging along."

"Dolph won't like it, at first. But I want you to talk to him, explain to him why you're sure Jassminsky was murdered."

"I could be wrong about all that, Carolyn."

"You aren't. You know you're right or you wouldn't have come here tonight," she said. "You're not the type of man who fools around, and that'd be the only other reason for visiting me."

"It's disheartening. Nobody thinks I'm capable of dallying."

Carolyn asked, "Will you come with me tomorrow night?"

Bert answered, "Yeah, I will."

# Chapter Six

*T*HE MAXIMUS COMICS, Inc. building in Manhattan rose nineteen stories above lower Madison Avenue. Most of the artists and editorial people were on the fourteenth floor, which was actually the thirteenth floor. After signing in at the reception desk and getting his stick-on visitor's pass, Bert made his way through the labyrinth of corridors toward the office where Juan Texaco was to be found from Monday through Wednesday.

A few of his old comic-book colleagues noticed him as he passed their cubbyholes and waved or groaned.

Outside Texaco's closed cubicle sat a very thin young woman in jeans and T-shirt. "What would you say my chances are?" she inquired, looking up from behind her desk.

"Of what?" Halting, he shifted his portfolio from under his right arm to under his left.

"Becoming a skin-magazine model."

"You want my honest opinion, as an artist and not a human being?"

"Are you an artist? I've only been here six weeks and still don't know all the people who—"

"I escaped several months ago. I used to draw the Human Beast."

Her eyes widened. "Then you must be Texaco's successful Connecticut friend he's continually boasting about when not trying to lay hands on me."

"Probably. I'm Bert Kurrie. Is he in?"

Wrinkling her nose, she answered, "Oh, yes, he's lurking in there. You going to lunch with him?"

"Intend to, yes."

"Takes all kinds." She shrugged one shoulder. "You were going to pass on your honest opinion of me."

"You're too slim," he told her. "Not that I personally don't like slenderness, but the men's magazine audience prefers—"

"Interestingly enough, you aren't the first person to mention that," the young woman admitted. "The problem is, I have an incredibly high metabolic rate. I burn up everything I eat. The amount of chow I put away would make the average woman impressively zoftig in less than a week and—"

"Quick, quick," urged Texaco, throwing open his door. "Duck in here, Bert, before you succumb to Daisy's siren song. Otherwise you'll end up taking her to lunch at some posh and expensive bistro, urging her to eat a massive meal in order to add a few pounds to her slatlike frame."

"Do they have a word for 'schmuck' in Spanish?" asked Daisy.

Texaco was making urgent come-in-here motions at Bert. "That's Daisy Ashford, the new art department associate secretary," he explained. "The city of New York made us take her on under the new Equal Opportunity for Nitwits Act."

Bert said, "Nice meeting you," and entered the cluttered little studio. "Another romance in the making, huh?"

"Shudder," said his friend, closing his door.

"No, I know your style, Texaco. The more you insult them, the more you are enamored."

"No man in his right mind would woo a lady who looks like a young Margaret Hamilton on a starvation diet." He seated himself at his tilted drawing board. "Besides which, how could any decent chap live through the shame of having his true love pose naked? And in Daisy's case, my friends and enemies alike would not only be able to ogle her most intimate portions, they could also count her ribs."

Bert rested his portfolio against the wall. Stuck up on this side of the room were proofs of comic-book pages Texaco had done, mostly of Flaming Death, the Human Beast, and Maximus's newest hit hero, KnightOwl. Scanning the work, Bert asked, "Who's inking your stuff now?"

"New fellow Carlotsky hired." Texaco picked up a pencil and tapped at his lower teeth with the eraser end. "Mayhap you know him. Name is Shaky Sankowitz."

Grinning, Bert lifted a pile of *Human Beast* comic-books off the room's only other chair and sat. "He's the guy who has to hold the brush in both hands to keep from quivering, isn't he?"

"No, you're thinking of Nervous Nolan, my former inker. This guy they have to lash to the board." Texaco sighed profoundly. "It's a tribute to the integrity of my penciling that even though Carlotsky keeps hiring half-wits who take this work to support their massive drug habits, the true worth of my art shines through. Yes, despite inking that—"

"What's that you're working on?"

Texaco turned his back to the page on the drawing board and held up a restraining hand. "Stay back, amigo. I don't want you to see how far I've fallen."

Craning his neck, Bert got a look. "Funny animals?"

"We're expanding our kid's line. Even though I screamed, threw myself at Carlotsky's mud-spattered boots, I still got stuck with Macho Moose and . . . you may not believe this when I tell you . . . I am also going to render the Carrots of Beanpole Street."

"Snappy title. What's it about?"

"Talking vegetables," said the cartoonist forlornly. "Did you ever try to draw breasts on an eggplant?"

"Only once, years ago."

"And how can you put legs on a carrot without making it appear obscene?"

"The artist's life is . . . no, wait. I've got an apter cliché. You've got a tough row to hoe."

"Don't let Carlotsky hear you talking like that or he'll make you editor of this produce extravaganza."

"How is my old boss?"

Texaco said, "When I chatted with him this A.M. he snarled in a loud, healthy way. My assumption is he's the same as always. Did you see your art director over at Mammoth Paperbacks?"

"Yep, and he okayed the rough."

"What are they paying for covers?"

"Two thousand dollars on this."

"Golly, if a feller could paint ten of them a month, he could live right handsomely."

"I'm averaging two so far."

"That's not bad, actually. Can I see the rough?"

"Sure." Bert opened his portfolio, fished out the drawing, and handed it across.

Texaco held the sketch at arm's length for a moment. "Have you ever considered doing this sort of thing professionally?"

"Nope, I have my heart set on a career as a nude centerfold."

"Me, too. We ought to team up." He rested the drawing on his lap. "Seriously, friend, this is damn good."

"I know."

"Getting out of here was a wise move."

"You ought to be able to do the same, now that you're working for Ty Banner and—"

"Soon. But don't talk about it too loudly. Carlotsky may discover the escape tunnel I've been digging." He stood up. "Chinese food today? There's a new place on Thirty-second. Called the MSG Pagoda or some such."

"I'd prefer something milder."

Stroking his chin, the curly-haired cartoonist said, "You have violent objections to that quiche joint on Twenty-eighth?"

"Not violent ones, no."

"We'll go there, then. They have a waitress who is a simulacrum for the youthful Mary Beth Hughes."

"Fine."

Texaco moved for the door. "Oh, by the way, what about that business you were talking about the other day? Was it murder or not?"

"I'll tell you about it at lunch."

"There's a hint of something ominous in your voice, my lad."

Bert said, "Well, I've talked to some people. One person actually, and she thinks there may have been more than one killing."

"Eh? You mean you're entangled in a series of violent deaths, the sort of thing Jack the Ripper brought off?"

"The girl thinks there've been two murders so far."

"So far? *Caramba*, as we say in my native land," said Texaco. "There's going to be more?"

"Right now I'm not sure," answered Bert. "I really don't have much in the way of facts to go on, but I ought to find out more tonight."

"Has it occurred to you that maybe you don't want to find out anything else?" asked his friend. "You might just wind up being victim number three or four."

His wife came into the twilit living room and found him crouched beside an open cardboard box. "Turn on a light."

"Hum?"

"That's what my father always used to advise." Jan clicked on the nearest table lamp. "According to him, the leading cause of blindness in America was reading without enough illumination."

"I was unpacking these books and came across this." Bert held up a slim paperback.

"*The Superhero Guide?* I bet that wasn't a Book-of-the-Month Club selection."

"It's what you call a fanzine, sort of. Somebody must've given it to me when I was up at Maximus." When he stood, his left knee produced a rusty-hinge sound. "One of the comic-book heroes they talk about is Captain Thunderbolt. Says here that Dolph Tunney used to work on the thing."

"And?"

Bending, Bert scooped up an armload of hardcovers out of the box. He carried the books over to the unfilled shelves built into the living-room wall. "You want to try for alphabetical order with these?"

"That's too stodgy."

"Okay." He deposited them on the shelf.

"But we might try to get them all right side up."

"Oops." He turned two books over.

"You think this man you were telling me about . . . Gruber, was it?"

"Mack Gruber, the guy who created Captain Thunderbolt back over twenty years ago."

"You think he's somehow involved in Beau Jassminsky's death?"

"Don't know." Tossing the fanzine on the glass-top coffee table he gathered up more books. "But what's interesting is how these guys all seem to be linked with Kreative Komics."

"Gruber got a lousy deal from that company?"

"That he did. His superhero precipitated the whole new boom. KK got rich; so did Maximus, DC and Marvel." He arranged the books on a shelf. "Gruber ended up with little money and a nervous breakdown."

"You can't blame a mental collapse on other people or on a company, though."

"You can't; Gruber might." One more armload emptied the box.

"What you're planning to do tonight," said Jan, sitting on the sofa. "Maybe, Bert, you shouldn't."

"Hey, I didn't know we had this. *Hollywood Character Actors.* Maybe I ought to study this, so I can communicate better with Texaco when—"

"My father gave that book to us. Bert?"

"Yes?"

"This Frame woman is having an affair with Dolph Tunney. That really isn't something you ought to mess with."

"It could be a little uncomfortable, but I'm going to do it."

"Suppose there really is a killer around loose? You—"

The phone rang.

Getting rid of the last of the unpacked books, Bert trotted to the nearest extension.

"Hello?" he said, leaning his backside against the desk in the den.

"My latest wife tells me you called, my boy. I've only got a few minutes, but I stand willing to help in my humble way."

"Listen, Ty, I can't quite explain what I'm up to."

"Adultery so soon?"

"No, no. This has to do with . . . anyway, I'm going to be meeting Dolph Tunney tonight."

After a few seconds of silence, Banner said, "Oh, so?"

"You know him quite a bit better than I do," continued Bert. "And you guys were at Kreative Komics together years back."

Banner asked, "This has something to do with Beau's death?"

"It might."

"Perhaps, old buddy," suggested the cartoonist, "you ought to let the local law do this sort of work."

"Listen, I'm not sure this ties in at all with—"

"You have a stubborn streak, a determination I admire," said Banner. "But this time you—"

"What sort of guy is Tunney?"

"A second-rate artist. He was damn smart to get into the art-supply trade," replied Banner. "Not a bad-looking chap, as he'd be the first to tell you. A devil with the ladies, as my old sainted grandmother might've said. If I'd had an Irish granny, which I didn't. Dolph used to booze it up a good deal in KK days, and I saw him go charging into a good many saloon brawls. I hear he's mellowed, but I wouldn't advise you to do anything that might annoy him."

"I'll make every effort not to."

"Would that I had time to stroll down memory lane with you the rest of the evening, Bertie," Banner said. "However, this is my night to attend my rap-group session and I must be off."

"Okay, thanks, Ty."

"One more thing," added Banner. "Be careful."

# Chapter Seven

*T*UNNEY'S SPRAWLING ranch-style house sat back on two wooded Westport acres. The drapes hadn't been drawn on the wide picture window, and you could see into the stark black-and-white living room. No one was visible.

Bert parked in front of the carport. "That his new Porsche?"

Nodding, Carolyn Frame said, "Dolph does very well."

"Apparently." He eased out of his car.

The blonde, who was wearing a simple cotton dress and sandals tonight, let herself out and went hurrying across the white gravel.

When Bert caught up with her, she was pushing the bell button. "He doesn't exactly know you're coming," she said. "So let me—"

"You didn't tell him you were dragging me here?"

"It'll be okay, once I explain." She jabbed the bell again and chimes bonged inside the big house. "Where the hell is he?"

Pines and evergreens walled the house from its neighbors. Bert heard faint classical music drifting from next door but couldn't see the house. "Maybe you should've prepared him for me."

"What have you heard about Dolph?"

"Nothing much."

"Oh." She poked the bell once more. "Some people say

he's hot tempered. I thought perhaps you'd heard that and were worried he'd punch you out or something."

"Is he likely to do that?"

"No, he's really a very gentle man. I, especially, bring that out in him, which is why . . . I don't understand why he's not answering." She dug into her purse and produced a ring with six jingling keys on it. "We'll let ourselves in, I guess."

"Okay."

Carolyn unlocked the door, opened it and pushed it, gingerly, inward. "Dolph? It's me."

"You talked to him today?"

"Yes, he phoned me just a couple hours ago. The coast is clear and he's expecting me," she said. "Dolph? It's Carolyn."

Bert frowned, sniffing. There was an odd warm, steamy smell coming out of the house. Edging around the girl, he went into the quiet house.

Two hallways led off the large living room. A black metal mobile was swaying very slightly, its jagged components looking like a flight of carrion crows.

"Dolph? Are you here?" Carolyn came into the white living room after closing the outside door carefully behind her.

At the end of one of the corridors a thin mist was swirling. Bert was aware of a gurgling, dripping sound from down there. "Stay here a minute, Carolyn."

"What is it?"

"Just wait right there." He moved down the hallway, fast.

At its end he nearly slipped and lost his footing. There was a slick of hot water on the hardwood flooring.

Swallowing once, Bert opened the bathroom door.

Steam came spilling out at him, spinning all around. The sea-blue carpeting was soggy. It made thick, slurping sounds as he crossed to the tub.

The hot-water faucet was on nearly full force; scalding water was gushing out. It hit the full tub, splashed. Water was sluicing over the pale green sides of the tub and splashing to the floor.

And there was a man in the tub. A big man, naked, his blond hair snaking around his submerged head and his eyes shut. The burning water hit at his body and splashed over the tub edge, hitting at Bert's shoes.

"Jesus," he said quietly. "Jesus."

Reaching to his right, he yanked a towel off the wall rack. Wrapping it around his hand, he turned off the faucet.

Stepping back, he found he was shivering.

He was nearly certain the man was dead.

"But suppose he's alive?"

Bert rolled up his shirt sleeves, took a deep breath. Then he reached into the water to take hold of the body. "God damn!"

He'd forgotten the water was going to be so damn hot.

"Is Dolph in here? What's—Oh, God!" Carolyn came rushing into the bathroom. "What's wrong with him? Get him out of there, you asshole. Why don't you pull him out of there?" She plunged her bare arms into the scalding water, grabbed hold of Dolph Tunney's arm.

"Take it easy, Carolyn. I think he's—"

"Shut up. Just shut the hell up." She was crying as she struggled with the big man's body. "Dolph, Dolph. What's wrong?"

"Careful, or—"

"Help me. Don't just stand there."

"He's dead, Carolyn."

"No, he's not. All we have to do is tug him free and use mouth-to-mouth—"

"Okay, I'll give you a hand."

They managed to get Tunney's torso clear of the water. When his upper body was draped over the tub edge, Bert put fingertips to his throat. "There's no pulse, Carolyn."

"Why do you keep saying things like that, you shithead? He's not dead! He's not dead! He's not dead! If you'll only help me—"

"You have to get out of here now. You can't do anything at all."

"But Dolph isn't dead." She was kneeling next to the tub, her right hand on the dead man's shoulder. "Don't you see he—"

"Carolyn, listen. That's just the way it is. I'm sorry, but he's gone." He caught her arm and pulled her up and away from Tunney.

"Christ, don't you have any heart? Why'd I ever bring an asshole like you here?" She was sobbing, shuddering, gulping in air. "All we have to do is give him—"

"He's dead." Bert pulled her nearer the doorway.

"He's not. He's not." The front of her dress was splotched with water and her blonde hair was tangled. "Why won't you help me? Please."

"I'll phone the police," he said quietly. "And you'd better call a doctor, too, huh?"

"Yes, for Dolph. That's a good—"

"For you, Carolyn."

"I don't need a doctor, asshole!" she shouted at him. "It's Dolph who—"

"Okay, okay." He put an arm around her wet shoulders and forced her out of the room. "Come on."

"He's just not dead," she said in a faraway voice, a brokenhearted little girl's voice.

Bert took one more look around the kitchen before turning off the lights. He went back along the hallway to the big black-and-white living room.

Carolyn was sitting in a black armchair, her hand resting on the phone. "I was hysterical," she said quietly.

"I know."

"Forgive me for calling you names. I sometimes do that when I lose control."

"Did you phone a doctor?"

"My attorney," she answered. "Did I mention my father's a very successful stockbroker? He is. And we have some very high-powered lawyers on call."

"Might help. What'd your lawyer say?"

"He's coming over."

"The cops might not like—"

"Oh, yes. They have to like whatever Sidney Lenzer does."

"Yeah, I've heard of him."

She asked, folding her hands on her lap, "What've you been doing?"

"Nosing around. There doesn't look to be any sign of a forced entry or break-in. None of the doors or windows have been futzed with."

"What do you mean?" Carolyn looked up at him.

"I was curious as to how the killer got in."

"My God." She pressed her right hand against her breast. "I forgot about all that. The list Dolph mentioned . . . he was on it, too."

"This could just be an accident, but—"

"No, it isn't," she said. "Damn, if he'd only told me more about what the hell was going on."

Bert asked, "Did he have an office or a studio here?"

She nodded. "An office, down the hall, next to . . . to the bathroom."

Bert went along the corridor. The steamy smell was thick in the air.

Tunney's office was small. There was a wooden desk, one filing cabinet, a portable electric typewriter on a stand. One wall was bookshelves, only half-used. There were old typewriter-paper boxes filled with tax and store records. A few framed photos on the other wall. Wife and children.

Bert sat in the desk chair. There was a half-filled coffee

cup sitting on a coaster. Cold. A baking-powder can full of pencils and marking pens, an appointment calendar.

*C-8PM* was the only notation on today's page.

"Wonder if his wife ever thumbed through this calendar."

He slid open the top drawer. Paper clips, rubber bands, a few fat manila folders. And a comic-book-sized pamphlet.

*Meet the People Who Bring You Kreative Komics,* the bold lettering on the cover invited.

Picking up the booklet, he noticed some newspaper clippings were being used as a marker. He opened the booklet and smoothed it out on the desk. The centerspread had a dozen photos and biographical paragraphs. *Meet Our 1962 Crew!*

Then Bert noticed the top clipping had a red 2 scrawled in its margin. This was an account, from the Norwalk *Hour,* of Beau Jassminsky's death.

"And what the hell's this?"

The other clipping was number 1. A week-old obituary notice from the *New York Times,* it dealt with the death of a man named Leon Brenner. Described as a New York-based editor of trade journals, Brenner, aged fifty-three, had died in his sleep in White Plains, New York, after a long illness. Bert had never heard of him.

Setting the clippings aside, he studied the pages they'd been marking. There among the staff photos Bert spotted Beau Jassminsky, more than twenty years younger, crew-cut and grinning.

"Yeah, and here's Leon Brenner."

Brenner was a thin, bespectacled man of about thirty and was then an associate editor at Kreative Komics. One of the magazines he worked on was *Captain Thunderbolt Comics.*

The last photo at the bottom of the page, just below that of a pretty dark-haired young woman, was that of a younger

Dolph Tunney. Back then, Tunney was "an ace inker in the KK bull pen."

Bert turned the page. More pictures and bios, including one of Ty Banner. No lines on his face then, no puffiness under the eyes and the hair not so thin.

One page more and he found Mack Gruber. Gruber was a big, blond, open-faced young man, smiling at the camera. The company gave him credit for "helping create America's favorite new hero—the one and only Captain Thunderbolt!"

Tires sounded on the gravel drive outside.

"They're here," called Carolyn.

Standing, Bert slipped the clippings back into the booklet. He hesitated, then folded it and slid it into a back pocket.

# Chapter Eight

"*T*HEY ALL LAUGHED?"

"It was more lack of interest than outright sniggering."

Jan was seated at the kitchen table, watching her husband pace. "You'd think the Westport police'd be more receptive to—"

"They weren't especially happy with Sidney Lenzer leaning on them." Bert paused by the sink to pour himself a glass of water. "The water's cleared up."

"It's less purple is all."

"See, there's Carolyn Frame all covered with bathwater and having a key to Tunney's house. It was awkward, and I think they'd have liked to ask more questions. But that attorney of Carolyn's has a lot of clout."

"Be that as it may, Bert, can't they see there's been a series of murders?"

"Sergeant Swanson, who was in charge of things tonight, is of the opinion we don't have a series of murders. Nope, what we have is two completely unrelated accidental deaths and a wiseass comic-book artist who's suffering from delusions."

"Didn't you explain you weren't in comics anymore?"

"He recognized my name because his younger son's a big Human Beast fan. To Swanson a comic-book artist is about two, maybe three, steps below a child molester."

"But there've been three murders." She tapped the borrowed booklet and the clippings, which he'd spread out on the kitchen table.

Bert finished his glass of water. "I didn't exactly mention Leon Brenner."

"Did you show them these darn clippings with 1 and 2 written on them? That's sure evidence of—"

"Evidence I've been ransacking Tunney's office," he said. "No, I didn't say a damn thing about Brenner. Especially after the way Sargeant Swanson reacted to my telling him there might be a connection between Beau Jassminsky's death and this one tonight."

Jan said, "It seems obvious that—"

"Look, maybe this Brenner guy did simply die in his sleep. The paper says 'a long illness.' That usually means cancer."

"Sure, and Jassminsky tripped and fell and this Tunney cracked his skull when he slipped in the bathtub."

"That's the simplest explanation." He was pacing again.

"Not necessarily the right one."

"Nope, I don't think so either. Tunney said 'Two down,' when he heard about Beau. He numbered these two obits. He himself turned out to be 3."

"How long is the list?"

Crossing, Bert picked up the Kreative Komics promotion booklet. "Right now there's no way of telling. If Tunney'd put numbers in here on some of the pictures, then there'd be something to go on. Could be he's the last in line, but it might also be every person in this thing is a possible target."

"I was going to suggest," Jan said, "that you might quit about now."

Rolling the booklet into a tube, he sat down opposite his wife. "That'd be the smart thing," he admitted, hitting the edge of the table with the booklet. "Don't annoy the Brimstone cops, don't annoy the Westport law."

"Don't annoy the killer."

"I guess, though, I'm not going to be smart."

"Didn't expect you were."

"I'm going to keep digging around," Bert told her. "See if I can at least find out the reason for this."

"You're worried about Ty Banner, too, aren't you?"

"Sure, his picture's in this thing and there's a good chance Ty's in danger as well," he answered. "Actually, I'd hate to see anybody get killed. Up until a few days ago, you know, I'd never even seen anyone who'd met a violent death. Now . . . anyway, Jan, I can't drop this. If I did and more people got killed, I'd feel responsible."

"You wouldn't actually be. The police are the ones who—"

"Yeah, but the least I have to do is come up with enough real information to get the cops interested. Then I can, maybe, drop out and let them go about their business."

"Where'll you start?"

"Tomorrow I'll talk to Ty Banner," he said.

# Chapter Nine

$T$Y BANNER'S STUDIO was large, orderly, and filled with afternoon sunlight. There were six neatly framed original drawings on the office walls and atop one of the three filing cabinets sat some of the awards he'd won over the years for his *Dr. Judge's Family* newspaper strip.

The cartoonist himself was sitting on a rattan couch with a portable drawing board resting on his knees. He was gazing out one of the wide windows toward the neighboring estate that rose up beyond a close-cropped acre of bright green grass. "Take a gander yonder, my boy, and tell me if I'm suffering from old-timer's disease," Banner requested, "or is that blonde wench on the tennis court naked."

Bert moved to a window, squinted. "I'd say she's playing tennis in a flesh-colored bikini."

Sighing, Banner said, "Ah, what's happened to the sport of Alice Marble?"

"Is that dark guy on the other side of the net your new neighbor, the one who designs video arcade games?"

" 'Tis he. Talk about getting rich quick. The bastard grossed eleven million dollars last month. Last *month*."

"Gosh, and you and I have to work a whole year to make that kind of money." Bert settled into a white wicker armchair, his back to the distracting blonde and facing his friend.

"I'll confess something to you." Banner put his board aside. "I'm losing papers. Nowadays the half-wit public wants humor strips like *Dribble* and *Poon County* and *Doomsberry* or whatever they're called. I read that garbage and can't even summon up a pained smile, my boy. Yet they're knocking out continuity strips, works like *Dr. Judge* that blend deft scripting with brilliant graphics. Hell, if I net a hundred thousand dollars this year I'll be damn lucky."

"I hear they've set up a soup kitchen in Westport."

"My boy, a hundred thou isn't big money any longer. Especially to a man paying alimony to a string of enough ex-wives to start a basketball team." He narrowed his eyes. "You sure that woman isn't jaybird naked?"

"Only nearly so."

"When you get up into your later fifties, you commence living in a fantasy world," he observed. "But you didn't come over here to listen to an old fart share his horny hallucinations, and since Texaco is only in residence in this sweatshop of mine on Thursdays and Fridays, you aren't here to see what sort of a taskmaster I am."

You could hear the tennis ball smacking the clay of the court. And the blonde laughing.

Bert said, "I guess you heard about Dolph Tunney."

Banner winced. "I was afraid that was going to be the object of your visit."

"Before we get into that, Ty, did you know a guy named Leon Brenner?"

"B.O. Brenner? Surely, he was an editor up at KK in the good old days," he answered. "Haven't thought of B.O. Brenner for years."

"B.O. for what, body odor?"

"Yes indeed, the lad really was fragrant. Not a bad editor long as you stood downwind of him. Or is that upwind? The object was not to get a whiff," said Banner. "How'd he get into this?"

"He died a week or so ago."

Frowning, Banner straightened up. "Old buddy, I am not fond of all these reminders of my own mortality. Hell, B.O. wasn't even as old as me."

"Paper said fifty-three."

"That's very young, youthful in fact. How'd he die?"

"Apparently from cancer."

"At least he wasn't tossed off a cliff or dunked in a tub," said the cartoonist. "That is your theory, is it not, that we're dealing with a screwball killer?"

"It must've been Tunney's idea, too." From his pocket he took the Kreative Komics booklet. He extracted the obituaries and handed them across to his friend. "I found these at Tunney's last night. The numbers seem to have been put there by him."

Banner scanned the clippings and then set them on the rug near his feet. "The implication is that Tunney's was death number three?"

"He sure seems to have considered that a possibility."

"What do the police think?"

"That he hit his head in the tub and drowned accidently."

"That simple and reasonable explanation doesn't satisfy you, my boy?"

"Nope."

"My local radio newscaster informed me that you and a lady named Frame found Tunney's body."

"I told you last night I was going to visit him."

"You failed to say exactly why."

Bert filled him in on Carolyn Frame and why they'd gone to Tunney's. "My feeling," he concluded, "is that something is going on, that none of these three deaths is accidental."

"Okay, maybe you can push a fellow off a cliff," conceded Banner, "and maybe you can hold him under water in his tub until he expires. But you can't give him cancer."

Bert shrugged. "Tunney had Brenner down as number one and Beau as two."

"What's that periodical you're clutching?"

"The obituaries were in this." He tossed the booklet.

"Ah, the past recaptured." Banner caught the booklet. "I haven't so much as seen a copy of this in years. I believe my wife before last burned my last copy during the year of the big freeze."

"I noticed you in there."

Banner was flipping through the pages. "Gad, this picture was taken during my matinee-idol phase. Imagine that, will you, only one chin and all that hair," he said. "Shocking how just two decades of dedicated boozing and broad-chasing can rob a man of his youth."

"Brenner, Jassminsky, and Tunney all worked up at Kreative while you were there." Bert leaned forward in his chair. "Do they have anything else in common?"

Banner thought about it. "Well, they were all involved in helping KK steal Captain Thunderbolt from Mack Gruber," he said finally. "Except that if he's getting revenge, he waited one hell of a long while."

"He was in a mental institution, wasn't he? He only got out recently."

"True, yet . . . ah, there he is." Banner had turned to Gruber's photo. "What an innocent face on the lad. He just radiates gullibility. 'Gorsh, fellers, here I am. Please take advantage of me right quick.' And, boy, did they."

"You talked to Gruber recently here in Westport. Did he sound like—"

"He seemed the same, only older and a bit subdued," answered Banner. "He sure as hell didn't confide any mass-murder schemes to me." He turned to another page. "Besides, old buddy, the chief culprit was old Guilfoyle here. He was the president of the whole Kreative shebang, and he made the biggest pile out of the screwing of Mack Gruber.

But he passed on to glory five or six years ago while chasing a nubile lass around the deck of his yacht while anchored in some exotic Caribbean port of call."

"Gruber could still be interested in revenge on the rest of them."

"Hum?"

"I said . . . what's wrong?"

Banner was looking at one of the small photos and shaking his head. "Haven't thought of her for a long time. She was much prettier even than this picture suggests." He leaned back, gazed up at the high white ceiling of his studio. "Yeah, Beverly Jepson. She did a lot of the early Captain Thunderbolt scripts. A damn good writer she was, could've reached the point where she was nearly as good as I am now."

"What prevented her?"

Banner made an unhappy gesture with his hand. "Boy, death is sure the topic of discussion this afternoon, folks," he said. "Bev killed herself years ago, right here in Westport. Funny thing was, she always seemed so sweet and innocent . . . nice. Do people of your generation use that word any more? Anyhow, she was the sort of girl you figured would marry once and make it work. She'd have four or five perfect kids and manage to write a few best-selling novels on the side. You expected to run into her years later and sigh, 'I don't know how you manage to do so much, Bev.' But instead she killed herself." Shutting the booklet, he dropped it to the floor. "That must've happened right after I quit KK, a couple months later at most. Long time ago."

"She can't have much to do with—"

"Wait now." Banner snapped his fingers. "Here's something odd."

"What?"

"Seems to me Bev's name came up recently."

"Where?" asked Bert.

Banner rubbed at his jawbone. "It was at one of our rap sessions. Right, that was it."

"So what was said?"

"I wasn't even at that particular session, having one of my rare deadline lapses. Just heard that she'd been mentioned from one of the other guys."

"It might be worthwhile to know what was said about her, since she used to work at Kreative, too," said Bert. "That is, if you guys can violate the sanctity of your sessions."

"Don't poke fun, sonny," said Banner. "Tell you what. If you really think it has anything to do with this muckraking mission you're on, you might go out to the University of Brimstone and talk to Warren Snyder."

"And he's who?"

"One of the fellows in our group, and I'm fairly sure he was at that particular session where Beverly's name came up," replied Banner. "He's a full professor in the English department now, but back twenty or so years ago, he was a young teaching assistant. He had Beverly in some of his classes, was her instructor I think. We've talked about her a couple times, long-ago mutual friend and all that."

"It's probably too far afield, but I may look the guy up."

"Give him a call, tell him I sent you," said Banner. "He ought to be fully recovered by now."

"Recovered from what?"

Grinning, Banner shook his head. "Seems that last night on his way to the campus parking lot to get his car the prof was waterbagged by some fun-loving students in one of the dorms. He didn't have time to change and arrived at the session a mite soggy."

"How come I didn't have fun like that in college?"

"Too busy pursuing coeds, no doubt."

"Actually I wasn't all that successful with women in my campus days."

"Unfortunately, I was. In fact, I went so far as to marry,

as the first of what has proved to be a lengthy series of wives, my college sweetheart. Don't ever do that."

"I'll try to avoid it." Bert got up. "Should you think of anything else, give me a call."

Banner gathered up the booklet and clippings and returned them to him. "I don't intend to think any further about this topic," he said. "Positive thinking is going to be my motto, and dwelling on the violent deaths of my contemporaries doesn't come under that heading."

# Chapter Ten

$T$HE NEXT AFTERNOON at a few minutes shy of two, Bert was walking across the University of Brimstone campus. The college's fourteen acres had all the traditional elements of a modest-sized New England center of learning— brownstone buildings rich with ivy, tree-lined lanes, a Gothic-style bell tower. The students he noticed roaming about, especially the girls, looked too young. He'd gone to college in California.

"Over a decade ago."

Professor Warren Snyder was teaching a class in American Lit in Plaut Hall. Bert, after asking directions from a young woman with what looked to be a punk haircut, found his way to the two-story brick building and climbed up to the second floor.

The door of room 203 was open. Glancing in, Bert saw a tall, lean, and dark-haired man of about fifty at the front of the room. He was lettering some names on the blackboard: Harlan Ellison, Frank Herbert, Larry Niven.

He lettered pretty well for a civilian.

The wall clock inside the classroom suddenly made a metallic jumping-ahead noise.

Professor Snyder said, "We'll continue on Friday. See you then, gang."

Chairs scraped, babble commenced. Fifteen or so students came hurrying out into the afternoon corridor.

After waiting a moment, Bert crossed the threshold. "Professor Snyder? I'm Bert Kurrie."

"Glad to meet you." He grinned, held out his hand. "As I mentioned on the phone last evening, I enjoy your work."

"The comic book stuff." Bert shook hands.

"There's good work to be found everywhere. In comics, paperbacks, even on television. You simply have to know how to look," the professor said. "It also helps to have what Hemingway called a built-in shit-detector."

Bert said, "I appreciate your seeing me."

"Well, I was intrigued." He shuffled papers into his briefcase. "I hope you won't think I'm being patronizing if I tell you I've never met an amateur detective before."

"I've never been one before," explained Bert. "This business, though . . . I've found two dead men and it made an impression on me."

"Let's walk over to my office, we can talk there." Snyder picked up his briefcase, moved to the doorway. "I take it the police don't share your belief that these were murders."

"Not conspicuously, no." He followed the professor out into the hall.

"And you believe Beverly Jepson figures in all this?"

"That I'm not sure of at all. Right now I'm just trying to gather together all the background information and see if I can make some sense out of it," he said. "Thing is, all three of the dead men worked up at Kreative Komics in the 1960s, and so did the Jepson girl. It might—"

"You mean two dead men, don't you?"

"No, a fellow named Leon Brenner died a week or so ago. Dolph Tunney seemed to think he was involved."

"You talked to Tunney about all this?"

"No, he was dead and gone when I got to his place."

They left Plaut Hall, started down a wide path.

"Beverly Jepson was an attractive and exceptionally bright girl," Snyder said. "One of the things I did when I was first here at UB, more than twenty years ago, was run a writing workshop for some of the more gifted students. The workshop wasn't official, merely something my youthful gung-ho self wanted to do."

"She was in the workshop."

"Yes, Beverly was the best writer in it," answered Snyder. "There was no doubt in my mind she was going to make it professionally. I'm a teacher, yet I also know there are some things you can't teach. She was a natural writer, with an exceptional talent. All I could do was try to guide her in the right direction."

"Did you guide her to Kreative Komics?"

Frowning, the professor shook his head. "She got the job on her own, shortly after she graduated," he answered. "My advice was that she was making a mistake, but Beverly saw it as a way to earn a living and be involved with publishing. I have to admit that some of the scripts she did were quite good."

"Did she move to New York City?"

"She stayed on with her parents. They had a home in Westport at the time. I never saw Beverly after she left college."

"That's not unusual."

"No, even your favorite pupils forget to come back." He laughed. "Now I'm sounding like my Jewish mother."

"Beverly Jepson died fairly soon after she left college and started at KK, didn't she?"

"A few months later and she was dead," he said. "Or so we assumed."

"Meaning what?"

Snyder nodded at a brick building on their left. "My office is over there," he said. "Beverly killed herself in a rather unusual way. I don't know, perhaps many people commit suicide in a similar manner. She . . . what they found were her clothes, neatly folded and piled, down on the beach in Westport one morning. There was a rambling note that asked every one to forgive her and didn't otherwise make much sense. She gave no reason for killing herself." He went up the marble steps, pushed open a door. "What Beverly did, you see, was swim straight out into the Sound. Apparently, so the authorities concluded, she swam out until she was too tired to swim any longer. Then she drowned."

"But her body was never found?"

"No."

The hallway was quiet and shadowy.

"She worked with three men that've died," said Bert. "Did she have anything else in common with them?"

The professor stopped at the door of his office, dug out his keys and unlocked it. "I probably ought not to discuss this with you," he said, entering the small office.

"You're referring to what came up about her at your rap session a few weeks ago?"

"We have more or less promised to keep what goes on there confidential." Snyder seated himself behind his cluttered desk. "Sometimes my students smoke during our conferences. That accounts for the odor in here."

Bert took the chair facing him. "I really don't know if what you guys talked about has anything to do with the deaths or not."

Snyder dropped his briefcase atop a stack of term papers on his desk. "Perhaps you may be able to do something to prevent further violence," he said. "I don't think the police would pay much attention to me, and frankly, because of my position here at UB, I would prefer not to approach them."

"The police and I, not in Brimstone and not in Westport, aren't exactly chums."

"Even so, you can do more than I can."

"If you tell me, yeah, then I—"

"This isn't a pleasant story." He folded his hands over his briefcase. "When I heard it a few weeks ago I was, having known Beverly, quite upset. I was, I suppose, frustrated as well. Since, at this late date, there's nothing much anyone can do."

"Do you think it has anything to do with what's going on?"

"We're not even certain what is going on, are we?" said the professor. "So there's no way to be sure. Do you know Fred Hibbard?"

"Vaguely. He lives in Brimstone and is what the advertising agencies call a decorative cartoonist. A pretty successful one."

"I don't detect much enthusiasm or admiration."

"Mostly I know his work, and he draws like dozens of other people. What about him?"

"Fred's in our rap group. He also once worked at Kreative Komics."

Bert said, "I didn't know that. During the same time as the others?"

"Yes." Leaning back, Snyder closed his eyes for a few seconds. "Over the past few weeks we've been covering the topic of guilt in our discussions. Things done in the past that produced lingering feelings of guilt, how to handle guilt, and so on. Hibbard, minimizing his own involvement, told us about the time twenty years ago when Kreative Komics was having a cocktail party in the office to celebrate some rises in circulation on their comic books. There was a young woman on the staff several of them found very attractive. She, however, wouldn't have much to do with them beyond a casual conversation now and then. So they slipped something into her drink, something that made her ill and dizzy. Then they took her to the apartment of one of them, which was nearby, pretending she could rest there and call a doctor. Instead they gang raped her. There were, I believe, six of them who took part."

After a few seconds, Bert said, "That was Beverly Jepson."

"Yes, and you must remember that twenty years ago our society was even less open about sex than it is now," Snyder said. "Even today, a woman who admits to a sexual assault is suspected of having asked for it. At any rate, Beverly never reported the men, didn't tell the police. Instead she quit Kreative Komics and stayed at home in Westport with her parents."

"Did she tell you about any of this?"

"We were student and teacher, not close friends," replied the professor. "I think that Beverly was a little uneasy about my advising her not to go to work up there in the first place. As I mentioned earlier, I never saw her after she left college. And, no, I didn't know she'd been raped."

"She killed herself soon after that?"

"Within a few weeks, yes."

Getting up, Bert walked absently over to a bookcase and glanced at a row of books without comprehending the titles. "Hibbard was one of the six. Did he name the five others when he brought this up?"

"My recollection is that he did. But since it was such an unpleasant narrative, I did my best to forget the details as soon as I could."

"Was one of them Beau Jassminsky?"

Frowning, Snyder rubbed at his chin. "Yes, he was."

"What about Tunney?"

"I'm not at all certain, although he may well have been mentioned," he replied. "The story gave me a shock and I didn't pay too close attention to the names he rattled off. Besides which, they were mostly men I'd never heard of before."

"So you don't remember if Leon Brenner was listed?"

"As far as I can tell, I heard his name for the first time when you mentioned the man today," Snyder said. "You know, she would've been a major American writer. There's no doubt in my mind."

# Chapter Eleven

$B$ERT PUSHED BACK from his drawing board. Locking his hands behind his head, he gazed up at the skylight above him. The day was waning and twilight was coming on with Maxfield Parrish flourishes. He stretched and returned his attention to the sketch he was working on.

This was a cover for a science fiction paperback. "I don't want hardware," the art director up at ZAP Books had told him. "I want mood."

So, Bert asked himself, not for the first time, what exactly is the mood of *Swordmaiden of Sandworld?*

"Dinner in about twenty minutes?" inquired Jan from the doorway of the studio.

"Hum?"

"Dinner. Twenty minutes."

He glanced over his shoulder at his wife. "Yeah, I guess."

"Problems?"

"Did you ever read anything by this Con Steffanson, who writes these Sandworld books?"

"No. I don't much like SF anymore, except for Frank Herbert."

"Art director gave me a photocopy of the first few chapters of the manuscript." He lifted up a sheaf of pages. "Plus some notes on the entire opus and proofs of the earlier covers. The novels seem to take place inside a grain of sand."

"That ought not to be too tough to draw. A single grain of sand."

Bert turned his chair around so he could sit facing the doorway. "I guess I'm preoccupied with the murders."

Crossing the room, she stood beside his drawing board. "Do you think it all ties in? The killings and what Professor Snyder told you this afternoon?"

"I'm not sure," he admitted. "Right now, several alternate possibilities occur to me."

"Such as?" She picked up the photocopied pages, started reading the first chapter of *Swordmaiden of Sandworld*.

Bert didn't speak.

"Well?" asked his wife.

"When you're through with Con Steffanson's majestic prose, I'll continue my—"

"I can listen and read at the same time. Really. You always assume—"

"Read the book, savor it and then—"

"All right, okay." Jan dropped the manuscript back on the board. "Did I mention you're much testier than usual?"

"Any further criticisms you'd like to air before—"

"Calm down," she suggested, backing up and sitting in an armchair. "It's not me you're ticked off at. It's either that cover or this murder business."

He took a deep breath and contemplated that. "You're right," he decided. "Sorry."

"Tell me what you were going to tell me."

He glanced upward again. The sky was darker and dusk was closing in. "The victims so far, and Beverly Jepson, all have at least one thing in common. They all worked at Kreative Komics in New York City in the 1960s. It is also possible all three of them were involved in the rape of the girl."

"But you're not sure of that part."

"Not yet, no."

"You plan to ask this man Fred Hibbard, who told the story at Ty's rap-session group?"

"Yep, but I have to approach him just right. Otherwise he may not talk to me at all," answered Bert. "I want to talk to Gruber, too."

Jan said, "A good motive for all this would be revenge, wouldn't it?"

"Sure, but for what?"

"Well, you've got Mack Gruber," suggested his wife. "Kreative more or less stole Captain Thunderbolt from him. He broods about that until he has a breakdown. When he's released, he decides to go after those who helped screw him out of millions of dollars."

"That's one possibility," Bert agreed. "A variation would be someone else who worked at KK and has a grudge."

"The tricky part is, why wait all this time to do something about it?"

"Could be I'm letting this KK link lead me astray."

"How so?"

"These three guys may have something else in common, something I don't know a damn thing about. All in the army together, all in the same college fraternity, all on the same bowling team."

"Or all raped Beverly Jepson."

"That's another possibility." Getting up, he commenced pacing the studio. "Again, though, why wait so long?"

"How about her parents? Might they—"

"Don't know where they are. Snyder told me they'd lived in Westport, but there's no one named Jepson in the phone book now."

She tapped her fingertips on the chair arm. "Here's a real left-field sort of idea, Bert. Suppose—"

"Suppose Beverly Jepson isn't dead?"

"Yes, exactly," she said, nodding. "It's farfetched admittedly, but still, they never found her body. Quite possibly she faked the suicide. Things like that have been done before."

"Where's she been the past twenty years?"

"We don't know that yet. Perhaps, ashamed and unsettled at what had happened, she went away. Changed her name, started a new life."

"Then one morning she wakes up and decides, 'Hey, I think I'll drop in on Westport and kill all those guys.'"

"Why not?"

"It's something I've thought about, but—"

"You're thinking of her as the girl in the picture in that brochure," said Jan. "But she's in her forties now, remember. For all we know, she's been living in this part of Connecticut for years. Put on forty pounds, dye your hair and you're not pretty little Beverly Jepson any longer. She could be someone you see all the time, the wife of some—"

"Still, there'd have to be something to precipitate the killings, nudge her into action after all these years."

"Maybe she's been someplace where she couldn't get out. A sanitarium, a prison." Jan sat up suddenly straight. "Or . . . or how about this? Leon Brenner, the first one, really did die of natural causes."

"And when Beverly reads his obit, that triggers something? She sees it, snaps and decides the rest of them ought to die now, too."

"Sounds plausible to me."

"When you start kicking theories around, everything starts sounding plausible," her husband said, returning to his chair. "That's the trouble with think tanking."

"I'm not claiming it's *the* answer, only one possible one."

"I agree that probably revenge is involved," he said. "But revenge for what?"

"You favor the notion it's Gruber, paying them off for his being cheated out of his creation?"

"Right now, Jan, the only way I could settle on one

specific notion is by tossing them all in a hat and plucking one out."

"Let's think about Gruber."

"Sounds like great fun."

"No, what I mean is, was he at that party?"

Bert stroked his cheekbone. "I don't know. I didn't think to ask Profesor Synder if Gruber's name had been mentioned at the rap session."

"Gruber might have been one of the six who raped her."

"I'll try to find out."

"Or," she said, "he might have been fond of her or even dating her. He didn't take part in the rape, but he found out about it. Revenge again, only this time for what they did to Beverly Jepson."

"Why wait so long?"

"Do you know how long Gruber's been in a mental institution?"

"Nope, but I don't believe it was twenty years. He didn't have the breakdown until a few years ago."

Jan rubbed her palms across her knees and stood. "I'll go get dinner presentable," she announced. "Ten minutes."

"Fine," he answered, not exactly sure of what she'd said.


The phone call came at a few minutes after 1:00 A.M.

The telephone was on the night table on Bert's side of the bed.

He wakened, sat up, and grabbed at the phone, heart thumping wildly. He got hold of it on the fourth ring.

"Hello?" he mumbled. With his other hand he groped until he grabbed the lamp switch and got the light on.

There was only silence on the phone.

Bert rubbed his eyes, squinted at his wristwatch that was sprawled on the table top. 1:09.

"Hello?"

"You don't know me," said a woman's voice.

Bert felt suddenly cold. Could this be Beverly Jepson phoning him? "I guess maybe I don't," he managed to say.

"Forgive me for telephoning you so late, Mr. Kurrie," the woman said. "I haven't been able to sleep very well since Dolph passed away."

"Oh, it's Mrs. Tunney."

"I felt I ought to speak to you," she said in a polite, tired voice.

"Well, sure. The thing is, Mrs. Tunney, it's late and—"

"I was out of town when it happened. We didn't get back until late yesterday. Tuesday afternoon, that is."

"Suppose I give you a call tomorrow? About—"

"You found Dolph, the police say."

"Yes, I did. I tell you, Mrs. Tunney, I'm not exactly too wide-awake at the—"

"Were you sleeping with her, too?"

"Beg pardon?"

"That whore, that Carolyn Frame bitch." The widow's voice remained calm and careful. "I knew Dolph was sleeping around with someone, but I wasn't sure who. In a way I learned something from his death. The name of the bitch he—"

"Maybe you ought to try to get some sleep, Mrs. Tunney. Call a doctor or—"

"Did you help her?"

"What?"

"Help her kill Dolph. She was tired of him and she wanted a new lover," said Mrs. Tunney in the same calm, weary voice. "So that slut and you broke into my house and killed my husband."

"We didn't have to break in, ma'am. She had a key." Bert hung up the phone.

Then he took the receiver off the hook again, set it carefully down next to the lamp. The phone talked to him for a few seconds, made some anxious beeps and then hummed softly.

72

"Bert?"

"I shouldn't have been nasty with her. But . . ."

"Who was that?"

"Dolph Tunney's wife."

"What did she want?"

"Nothing much," he said. "She just wanted to accuse me of murdering him."

# Chapter Twelve

$W$HEN THE PHONE in his studio rang at ten the next morning, Bert just sat staring at it.

On the other hand, it might be a client.

He left his board, shuffled over to the brick-and-board bookshelf where the phone was sitting.

"Hello."

"Did she phone you last night?"

"Is that you, Carolyn?"

"Yes, sorry. I'm a bit unstrung. Did that old bitch phone you at some ungodly hour?"

"If you're referring to the widow Tunney, yes."

"Accused us of murdering Dolph and being lovers, for Christ's sake?"

"Yep."

"Well, damn it, I don't have to put up with that kind of crap. I'm going to get Sidney Lenzer and we'll sue her ass off for slander and—"

"Whoa now," he suggested quickly. "This is a situation, seems to me, that calls for an extremely low profile."

"This woman accused me of killing Dolph, of having an affair with you, of—"

"She'll get over it."

"Will she? Dolph told me all about her," said Carolyn. "She's a bloodless, vindictive shrew. She made his life a—"

"Husbands who're fooling around aren't always the best and most reliable witnesses."

"Whose side are you on, anyway?"

"Listen, the best way to get Mrs. T. off our backs is by finding out who really killed Dolph."

"Maybe so, but it really pisses me off that—"

"Dolph Tunney died and it's upset both of you. His wife is just reacting in her own way."

After a silence, Carolyn asked, "Are you making any progress?"

"Some."

"Can you tell me about it?"

"Not yet," he said. "How are you faring?"

"Oh, I'm okay. I'm back working at the paper. In fact, I'd better get off the phone," she told him. "Thanks for listening to me, Bert."

"Part of our service. Bye." He hung up, went back to his drawing board. "I wish I was really as calm and unworried as I just pretended to be."


"Decisions like this," explained Texaco, "are important and mustn't be hurried."

The hefty brunette waitress tapped her pencil on her pad. "Your friend is a little bizarre," she observed to Bert.

"That's why I rarely take him out in public."

The curly-haired cartoonist shut his Riverside Diner menu. "I have reached a decision," he announced. "Stuffed cabbage, home fries, carrots, and a medium 7-Up."

"What sort of dressing on your salad?"

Texaco stiffened. "I'll have to think that over."

"Is he an artist like you?" the waitress asked Bert.

"Yes, but vastly inferior."

Texaco said, "Russian dressing."

"We don't have it."

"French?"

"You got it."

"Hope Emerson," said Texaco, watching her lumber off.

"There was a 1940s movie queen who looked like Rita?"

"Not a queen exactly." He twisted in his booth seat, scanning the long narrow diner. "So this is one of the gourmet meccas of Westport, eh?"

"It's cheap for lunch."

Texaco said, "My two days out here with all you white folks are working out pretty well. Assisting Ty isn't hard, and I can make it to Westport on the train in a shade over an hour."

"Usually."

He grinned. "You locals all bitch and moan about the Metro-North trains," he said. "But, amigo, after the NY subways, it seems like the celestial express. Although I do miss the graffiti."

"How's the Carrot Family coming?"

"Hey?" Texaco cupped his hand to his ear.

"Your talking-vegetable comic book."

"This is Thursday, is it not?"

"Far as I've been able to determine."

"Good, because Thursdays and Fridays I labor on *Dr. Judge's Family* and think not of far-off Maximus Comics, Inc."

"Forgive my mentioning it."

"I did work out a nice sequence wherein an artichoke does a striptease, but Carlotsky shot it down." Texaco slouched. "Are you still sleuthing?"

"I don't think I can afford to quit."

"How come?"

"Dolph Tunney's wife has the idea that Carolyn Frame and I snuck into her house and held him under the water."

"What was your motive, may I ask?"

"I'm Carolyn's other lover and she got tired of Tunney."

"That's an excessive way to end a relationship. If my old flames did things like that, I'd be dishpan hands all over by now," he said. "By the by, what's this Carolyn look like?"

"Audrey Long."

"That's not bad, since . . . huh?" He straightened up, eyes widening. "Since when do you compare contemporary ladies to long-ago screen lovelies?"

Bert laughed. "I happened to come across a book about actresses of the 1940s."

"Audrey Long was quite cute, made some fair B movies and . . . does your Carolyn really look like her?"

"They're both blonde."

"I ought to meet her, then. Blondes, especially middle-class intelligent ones, are fond of dallying with swarthy Latins."

"I hadn't noticed."

"Neither have I. But I read that in a high-school sociology book once. Downward mobility, they call it."

Bert decided to drink some of his ice water. "This whole case has—"

"Salads," announced Rita, setting both bowls down in turn.

"Your name is truly Rita?" Texaco asked her. "It isn't a nickname?"

"My real name. Why?"

"I thought perhaps you were nicknamed that because of your striking resemblance to Rita Hayworth of the cinema."

"The last time I saw a picture of her in the *National Intruder* she didn't look that nifty to me." She withdrew from their vicinity.

"Flattery," explained Texaco. "One of our great weapons in the arsenal of democracy. You was saying?"

"I've come across quite a lot of new information since you and I talked last."

Texaco poked at his salad with his fork. "Are tomatoes supposed to have legs?"

"No more than four."

"That's okay then. What sort of information, pertinent stuff?"

"That's what I'm trying to decide." Bert gave his friend an account of what he'd learned from Professor Snyder.

When he finished, Texaco observed, "That is not a heart-warming narrative. You think any of today's Maximus gang would do something like that?"

"Rape hasn't gone out of fashion."

"True, yet chaps in the funny-book trade have a certain code," he said. "Much like the Knights of the Round Table."

"Anyway, it happened then and all three of the guys who've been killed may've taken part."

"Have you asked Ty if he remembers any of this?"

"Not yet. I thought I'd do some more digging first, talk to Mack Gruber, try to track down Beverly Jepson's family, approach Fred Hibbard," said Bert. "Problem is getting near any of them. These aren't topics, rape and murder, that everybody's eager to chat about."

"I don't know about the others, amigo, but you ought to be able to hit Gruber tomorrow night."

"Where?"

"Ty tells me that some of the local artists and the staff of Artist's Workshop where Beau Jassminsky worked are planning to throw an informal memorial service for Beau tomorrow night."

"Cartoonists' wakes can be rowdy affairs."

Texaco shrugged. "Better than crying in your beer," he said. "This one'll be at the Shore Edge Country Club here in Westport. Ty's contemplating attending, and he says Gruber's been invited and has accepted."

"Want to go?"

"Nay. I have a date in the Apple mañana eve. This woman looks exactly like the Lane Sisters."

"Sounds bulky."

"You can tag along with Ty."

"Yeah, I'll do that."

"Deeper," said Texaco.

"Hum?"

"You're getting in deeper and deeper."

# Chapter Thirteen

"*A* NECKTIE?"

"It's a wake, after all."

Jan took several steps back from her husband, tilted her head to the left, and watched as he tied the necktie at the bedroom mirror. "I'm wondering, though, if yellow with red polka dots is exactly right."

"It's a cartoonist's wake."

Smiling, she sat on the edge of their bed. "Did you see the phone messages I left pushpinned to your drawing board?"

He turned from the bureau mirror so he could look at her rather than her reflection. "More threats and accusations?"

"Nope, mostly business. Les Free at Apex Books wants you to call him first thing Monday."

"Oh, so? Has he got an assignment for me?"

"He asked me if you could draw boats. That's the only clue."

"What'd you tell him?"

"That if you couldn't draw it, you could swipe it."

"That's our motto." He crossed to the closet and reached into its shadows. "Anything else?"

"Some people want you to go to New Haven Sunday."

Bert decided to wear his darker brown sport coat. "What do they plan to do to me once I arrive?"

"It's a comics convention, fans and dealers and all that."

"I'm out of comics."

"Yes, I informed them, but . . ."

"But what?"

"The plump young man who phoned . . . I assume he was a plump young man since he had a plump young man's voice."

"Most comics fans are plump young men."

"He told me they had arranged to have Kris Asanovic as their special guest on Sunday, except he had to go to the hospital and—"

"Kris? What's wrong with him?"

"Pneumonia. He's doing well, but has to stay in for a few more days."

"It's his damn life-style. What hospital?"

"Someplace in Hartford. I didn't ask. I wasn't aware you were that close."

"We're not. But he's only twenty-two . . ."

"He told the plump young man your stuff influenced him when he was a kid."

"Yeah, when we were both up at Maximus," admitted Bert as he got the coat on. "It was sort of refreshing to see somebody who hadn't been inflenced by Jack Kirby, Gil Kane or Neal Adams."

"This young ailing disciple of yours told the alleged fat boy that you could maybe fill in for him."

"Hell."

"You don't have to."

"What time?"

"They said if you could be there from noon to three, it'd be marvelous."

"Where?"

"The Bulldog Motor Lodge in New Haven."

"Sounds like my kind of place. We weren't planning anything special Sunday?"

"No, and I took down the instructions on how to get to

the place. Assuming your soft heart would compel you to attend."

"The poor kid's in the hospital."

"What about your own work?"

"I'm ahead on my deadlines," he assured her. "Despite the time I've been devoting to sleuthing."

"You sound like you're not making much progress."

"What I feel is that I'm not moving fast enough," he said. "There could be another murder in the works and I may not be in time to stop it."

The Driftwood Room of the Shore Edge Country Club faced inland. From its triptych of high wide windows, you looked out on the golf course and a wooded area beyond.

Twilight was giving way to darkness as Bert turned away from the bar and returned to the spot where he'd left Ty Banner standing.

Banner was talking to a gray-haired man in slacks and gold sweater. "You know Bud Heinz, don't you?"

"Sure. Hi, Bud. How's *Seaweed Sam* doing?"

"We lost two more damn papers," answered the cartoonist. "If they didn't love the damn strip in Europe I'd be selling apples on a street corner."

"Nobody does that anymore, old buddy," said Banner, sipping his martini.

"Sure they do, only nowadays you have to have organic apples or . . . Hey, there's Jerry Marcus. Want to talk to him about setting up a poker game. See you."

"Sad days for the comic strip," observed Banner after Heinz left them. "A classic like *Seaweed Sam* is failing, a gem of purest prose and art like my inimitable *Dr. Judge* is faltering."

"Better stock up on apples."

"Ah, the cruelty of youth."

"I'm in my thirties, that's middle-aged."

"No, no. Fifty-five is middle-aged. Anything under forty is callow youth."

Bert was looking around at the fifty or so people, mostly men, who were gathered around the dimlit room. "Is Mack Gruber here yet?"

"Not yet, Philo."

"Fido?"

"Philo, as in Philo Vance. A dapper detective often portrayed upon the silver screen by William Powell."

"Texaco is having an effect on you."

"William Powell was not a 1940s starlet," said Banner.

Bert drank some of his Perrier. "There's a formal part to this?"

"In a half hour or so they'll make a few little speeches about Beau, toast his memory, and then return to serious boozing."

"Did most people like Beau?"

Banner said, "I doubt it, my boy, but when one of your colleagues passes on, you turn out to pay your respects. Cartoonists, and even some of the more legit artistes like you, are a slobbery sentimental bunch at heart. Don't let the glossy, sophisticated exteriors con you. Most of 'em cry at weddings, go 'Ooh!' over baby pictures."

"I knew you were like that down deep, but . . . Hi, Mel."

A cartoonist strolled by, waved, and continued on his way to a cluster of people in a shadowy corner.

"Are you still actively investigating Beau's demise?"

"His, Tunney's, Brenner's."

"Conclusions?"

"None yet."

"I haven't had much chance to talk to you since you dropped in on Warren Snyder. You saw him, didn't you?"

"Yep, he brought up quite a bit of stuff about . . . Isn't that Gruber coming in?"

Banner checked the doorway some twenty yards away.

"It is, my boy. He looks damn good for a fellow who's been through what he has."

Mack Gruber was a tall, broad-shouldered man in his fifties. Tan, his blond hair wavy. He wore a dark suit, a gray striped tie. For a moment he hesitated in the doorway. Then, noticing Banner, he grinned and headed over.

"Mack, my boy." Banner shook hands. "Would that I looked as fit as you."

"Start lifting weights instead of martini glasses." Gruber nodded at Bert. "You must be Bert Kurrie."

"I am." They shook hands.

"I liked what you were doing at Maximus. Shame you quit."

"Not from my point of view. I'm a hell of a lot happier doing paperback covers and—"

"Happy, that's the thing to be. Money's nice, too, but happy is better," said the big, blond cartoonist. "Still and all, Bert, that work you did on the Human Beast was damn good. Now, the character's stupid and the plots are inane. I know you didn't write that crap and your drawing is what saved it. Layouts, staging, storytelling. Great."

"Thanks. I didn't know you kept up with—"

"With comic books while I was in the loony bin? Sure, I could read anything I wanted. Although I had to shave with an electric razor."

"I didn't mean—"

"I don't try to hide anything. I had a breakdown, I got better. No worse than a bad cold."

"I believe I'll refill this with vegetable juice." Banner held up his empty glass and started toward the bar.

"He used to be a good artist, too," remarked Gruber.

"Ty's still damn—"

"He's lazy now. I see his strip every day and the dang thing annoys me. See, Bert, I know what he can do." Gruber tapped his chest. "What can really foul you up is being good and not living up to it. Ty's using all those shots of buildings that he's just swiping from photos. And a bunch of talking heads most days. You've got to keep exercising your brain as well as your body."

"Are you still drawing?"

"I'm working on a new feature right now." Gruber paused, stared out at the dark golf course. "I understand you think Beau was murdered."

"How'd you hear—"

"I keep my ears open, talk to people. Read a lot. I take an active interest in what's going on, although my dear sister thinks I'd be better off sitting out on the patio and watching the dang Sound for a few months. Life's too short as it is, and I lost nearly four years in the hatch. Haven't got any more time for sitting on my butt."

"Had you seen Beau since you've been in Westport?"

"Once or twice, just briefly. I was over to that second-rate Artist's Workshop joint once, too," replied Gruber. "I had a terrific idea for a new way to teach cartooning by mail. Those half-wits weren't interested at all."

"Can you think of any reason for someone's killing Beau?"

Gruber laughed. "Hell, I can think of dozens, Bert," he said. "He was always trying to move in on someone's wife or lady friend. He was an arrogant loudmouth, a mediocre artist, and if you loaned him money you wouldn't see it back for years. Had I been God, I might have tipped Beau off that cliff just to get rid of one of my mistakes. Scrap him and back to the old drawing board."

"You going to be saying something along those lines tonight?"

"Not going to say a dang thing. There's enough people here to make politer speeches," he said. "These things are more like roasts than wakes anyway. You think Dolph Tunney was murdered, too?"

"He sure didn't slip and hit his head. Somebody drowned him."

Gruber said, "Death is breaking up that old gang of mine."

"Matter of fact, I'd like to talk to you about the time when you worked up at KK."

"You sound like you're planning a fanzine article."

"I've been trying to get information on—"

"Hell, I like to talk about the good old days," Gruber told him. "Guilfoyle and those other bastards up there cheated me out of something like twenty-seven million dollars so far. That's counting what the company's taking in on the new Captain Thunderbolt movie. Even so, I bear no ill will. Happy as a clam, that's Mack Gruber. Took near to four years in the funny farm to reach that plateau, and I'm not climbing down. I figure I can create something new and make my own twenty-seven million. Give or take a million or two."

"When can we—"

"I'm free tomorrow, Saturday, all afternoon. Drop over to my sister's mansion. It's not far from here." He took out a blank card and neatly printed an address and phone number. "Always do my own lettering and inking."

Bert accepted the card. "Around one okay?"

"Be looking forward to it. Now I think I'll go over and say hello to Mort Walker. That ought to cheer him up. See you tomorrow."

"Tomorrow," echoed Bert. He looked at the card again and then put it in his coat pocket.

# Chapter Fourteen

$T$HE DISTANT SAILBOATS were small white triangles on the Sound.

"I never have been out on one of those things," said Mack Gruber.

He and Bert were sitting on a wide flagstone patio behind the sprawling white mansion. Beyond the gently sloping acre or so of grass was a low brick wall. Then a drop down to a slice of sandy beach a hundred feet below. After that came the quiet blue of the Sound.

Bert looked away from the water and back at the two pages of artwork the cartoonist had brought out to show him. "This looks pretty good," he said truthfully.

Gruber was still watching the sailboats glide across the calm water. "All my own work. Pencilling, inking, lettering," he said. "And I wrote the damn thing, too."

"You plan to show this to DC or Maximus or—"

"Hell, no." Gruber laughed. "Going to publish the dang thing myself." He moved his deck chair some, leaned toward Bert. "I didn't vegetate while I was in the goofy farm, Bert. I kept up with all the developments in the field, subscribed to the *Comics Journal, Buyer's Guide, Comic Reader* and read every page, every line. Now, in the past few years there's been, as you probably know, a real growth of what they call the alternate press. Independent publishers, kids a lot of them, who don't have the overhead or the pigheadedness of the big outfits like Kreative Komics. Doesn't cost that much to print, say, fifty thousand copies of a comic book and then deal directly with comics shops or the distributors who cater to them. There's hundreds of these comics shops around the country, more springing up. Sure, some'll go down the drain and lose all their money. Most will survive, though. You sell your comic book outright, for 30 or 40 percent of the cover price, and you don't have to worry about returns. Guys like Jack Kirby are working for outfits like that and seem to be doing okay. I'm nearly as well known as Jack, and since my dear sister is going to bankroll me, I've decided to produce and distribute *Ms. Tique* myself. A feminist superheroine ought to do dang well about now."

"Anything done this well ought to sell."

"You can sell on the artwork alone once maybe, Bert. But I'm aiming for six issues a year, year after year," explained Gruber. "Followed by spin-offs, albums, novelizations, T-shirts, even a movie or two."

Bert set the originals on the metal-topped table between them. "When'll you be ready to start?"

"I already have my printer lined up. I'll have the whole thirty-two pages of my first issue finished in about three weeks," Gruber said. "But, you know, Bert, I don't think you dropped in this afternoon for chitchat about Mack Gruber's sensational comeback."

"I've gotten interested . . . involved is maybe a better word . . . in the murders of Beau Jassminsky and Dolph Tunney."

"Second-rate artists, both of them," observed Gruber. "Dang lucky they got themselves steady jobs. Tunney drew some Captain Thunderbolt stories when it got to where there was too much for me to handle. Even by swiping me he couldn't turn out anything worth a damn. KK had seven different titles with the captain going for a time. Hell, they still have three." Picking up one of his drawings, he rested it across his lap and studied it. "The newspapers claim Beau simply took himself a fall."

"I don't think so."

"And Dolph drowned after slipping in the tub."

"With Tunney, I don't have any proof it wasn't an accident," admitted Bert. "But he'd told someone that Beau's death and Leon Brenner's were—"

"Old B.O." Gruber chuckled.

"Tunney thought their deaths were linked. When I went over to talk to him about it, I found him dead, too," said Bert. "That's stretching coincidence too damn far."

"What did Dolph think was the reason for all this slaughter?"

"I don't know, since I never got the chance to talk with him."

"Inconsiderate of him to die before briefing you."

"All three of these guys worked at KK, same time you did."

Laughing, Gruber said, "I see it all now. Mack Gruber, crazed cartoonist, escapes from loony bin and murders all the bastards who were in on screwing him out of Captain Thunderbolt."

Bert watched the big blond man's face for a few seconds. "It's one possibility," he said finally.

Gruber nodded. "Five years ago, before I cracked up," he said slowly, "I was crazy enough, and angry enough, to have tried that maybe. I really did hate just about everybody who worked up there. Not now."

"You knew all of them. Can you suggest—"

"Ever hear of a girl named Beverly Jepson?"

Bert answered, "Yes."

"You know what happened to her?"

"She killed herself."

Gruber pointed toward the water. "Wasn't too far from

here," he said. "Beverly was a nice girl, pretty and on the shy side. Her scripts for Captain Thunderbolt weren't as good as mine, but she had a lot of talent."

"Were you at that party?"

"For a while, yes. But I left before they pulled their stunt on Beverly and doped her," he answered. "There were six guys in on that deal, and they had to get themselves pretty drunk before they had the nerve to go ahead with it. I never found out what really happened until quite a while afterwards. She quit, never told anyone."

"Suppose she'd gone to the police? It would've meant jail."

"No, they had her fairly well figured out," Gruber told him. "Sensitive, intelligent girl, lived with her parents. And this was twenty years ago. The odds were in their favor that Beverly wouldn't blow the whistle on them. And she didn't. Instead she just left KK, kept quiet, and then obligingly killed herself."

"How'd they react to that?"

"Six different ways, but I wouldn't guess any of them contemplated entering the priesthood or joining the Peace Corps to atone for his sins," said Gruber. "They were fairly young, some of them not too smart. It didn't bother most of them that much. You rape a girl and a few weeks later she kills herself. That's her problem. You have to have brains before you can crack up the way I did."

Bert asked him, "Do you know the names of all six?"

"Couple years after it happened, Hibbard and I got drunk together one evening. He spilled out the whole thing. Details, names. Half-remorseful, half-bragging. That's how the guy is." Shifting in his chair, Gruber tugged a small notebook from the hip pocket of his denim slacks. "Sure, I knew every dang one of them. I'll give you a list, since it might just come in handy."

While the cartoonist lettered the names, Bert gazed out

at the Sound. Was Beverly Jepson still out there some-where? And what would be left of her after all these—

"Here you go, Bert." Gruber tore the page free and handed it to him.

The list said:

Leon Brenner
Dolph Tunney
Beau Jassminsky
Marvin Appel
Fred Hibbard
Ty Banner

# Chapter Fifteen

*A* MILD SPRING RAIN was drizzling down on the parking lot that ringed the Bulldog Motor Lodge. Bert sat in his car for a few minutes after parking, gazing at the three-story pink plaster building.

"I'll have to talk to Ty about it," he said to himself. "Should've done that yesterday right after Gruber gave me that list of names."

The motel was not in the academic sector of New Haven and was surrounded by other motels and fast-food restaurants. There was, though, a Yale Diner across the way.

"He would've told me he'd been one of the guys who raped Beverly Jepson."

Bert had known Ty Banner for several years, and while not intimate friends, they were sure fairly close acquaintances.

He sighed out his breath, got out of his car. Sprinting, he moved through the noon drizzle to the entrance of the big motel.

He noticed two plump young men in jeans and T-shirts walking toward a corridor that led off the maroon-and-gold lobby. Not bothering to inquire at the desk for the location of the comics convention, Bert trailed the two youths.

Sure enough, they led him to a card table next to the entrance of the Nutmeg Ballroom. The slightly lame table was manned by a plump young man who was taking the dollar admissions while eating a wedge of cold pizza.

"I'm Bert Kurrie," he informed the gatekeeper.

The youth blinked, sat up, wiped his mouth with the back of his hand. "That's great," he said, chuckling. "Great. You're Bert Kurrie."

"That's me, yep."

"Boy, I love you."

Bert grinned. "Thanks. I'm supposed to—"

"I hope you won't mind my telling you that you're making a bad mistake."

"How so?"

"Quitting Maximus," the chubby young man explained. "That was a dumb move, Mr. Kurrie. The *Human Beast* was, let's face it, your finest hour. It defined the parameters of your talent. Can I be frank with you?"

"Fire away."

"The paperback covers you're trying to do, the few I've seen so far, are pure crap."

Nodding, Bert said, "It's always nice to get the man in the street's view of—"

"Need the money, I suppose? That's why you're attempting to crack the book market."

"Yeah, I have a lot of vices," confided Bert. "Couldn't support them on the Maximus wages."

"It's happened to better men than you," the youth said with sympathy. He opened a stamp pad, whapped a rubber stamp into it. "Let me stamp your hand so you can get in and out with ease, Mr. Kurrie. Forgive the fact that our rubber stamp says St. Norbert Church Wednesday Bingo. Someone swiped our ConComixCon stamp." He printed, in purple, the slogan on the back of Bert's left hand.

"Doesn't offend my basic religious beliefs," said Bert. "Can you tell me where to find Leroy Henkel? He's the one who invited me to—"

"I'm Leroy." He held out his plump hand. "A real pleasure meeting you."

"Same here. What am I supposed to—"

"Rosco!" shouted Henkel, looking back into the ballroom. "Rosco'll show you to your table."

There were roughly two dozen tables around the motel ballroom. Most of them were piled with comic books, boxes of comic books, paperbacks, and assorted magazines. There were bright posters taped to the walls, including one of the Human Beast that looked to be Bert's work. He had no recollection of ever having done it. Forty or so people, most of them plump young men, were browsing and socializing amid the rows of tables.

"What am I supposed—"

"You haven't attended many cons?"

"Not too many, no."

"You sit at your table for three hours. We've got a sketch pad and some markers for you, if these louts haven't swiped them already," explained Henkel. "You can draw sketches of the Human Beast, sign autographs, whatever. If you want to charge for the drawings, you can keep all the money from—"

"Nope, I'll donate my time."

Henkel shrugged. "Would you like me to get you a pizza?"

"A glass of water'll do."

"Tell Rosco. Rosco!"

A lean, bearded young man of twenty appeared on the threshold of the dealers' room. "Is this him?"

"Right, Rosco. It's Bert Kurrie."

Rosco smiled broadly. "You're great, Mr. Kurrie. You know, I feel you're nearly as good as Steve Ditko or Juan Texaco."

Bert looked modestly down at his shoes. "Ditko maybe, but never Texaco."

"Modesty never gets you anywhere in this business."

Rosco escorted him through the room to a card table in the far corner. Taped to the wall near it was a hand-lettered poster proclaiming: BERT KURRIE! Here At Noon! Maximus's STAR cartoonist!

"I always knew, if I kept at it, I'd be a star," said Bert as he squeezed himself into the chair behind the table.

"How about Baxter paper?"

"Well, since I no longer—"

"What about KnightOwl's killing that troop of Boy Scouts in number eleven and number twelve?"

"I don't see many comic books since—"

"Do you feel the killing and violence in Maximus Comics is a result of—"

"How about when Blazing Death ignited Helen and she burned to a crisp and then the League of Super Avengers voted to suspend his superpowers for—"

"I missed that issue because I no longer—"

"Yeah, but he cried when he scattered her ashes over Long Island Sound."

"He was faking."

"Mr. Kurrie, Mr. Kurrie, are you going to draw the Human Beast graphic novel?"

"Nope, I'm completely out of—"

"About printing on Baxter paper as opposed to printing comics on Mando paper? Don't you think the color contrasts are—"

"Mr. Kurrie, Mr. Kurrie, will you autograph this?"

"What is it? A paper cup?"

"I can't afford to buy any of the old *Human Beast* issues you drew. See, I'm in college and my mother has terminal—"

"He spends all his cash on coke."

"Like hell. You fat-assed—"

"Fellas," suggested Bert to the dozen young men circling his table, "let us strive for some semblance of order." He

98

signed his name on the paper cup with one of the felt markers he'd found scattered at his table.

"What do you think of the Princess BloodLust miniseries that Kreative Komics is doing?"

"Haven't seen it."

"Do you like Frank Miller?"

"Do you think KnightOwl's refusal to get treatment for his social disease will make him less effective against the Universe Two invaders, especially Darkthot who—"

"I tell you," said Bert, "I really haven't kept up with—"

"In *Tales of Blood* number 232 and number 233, Mr. Kurrie, you drew the Human Beast yarn entitled *I Have No Mouth Yet I Must Holler!* Why did you draw the Statue of Liberty with the wrong arm holding up the torch?"

"Did I?"

"But it was a dream sequence," said another fan. "Therefore—"

"It wasn't Alternate Earth Three," pointed out yet another young man. "So the usual mirror reversals wouldn't be—"

"Mr. Kurrie, Mr. Kurrie, will you sign this?"

"What is it?"

"My pizza box. I can't afford to buy your—"

"Isn't Baxter paper better for certain—"

"What about Ty Banner?"

"I don't think he was one of the six." Bert shook his head, looked up at the puzzled young man who'd asked the question. "Excuse me, I was thinking about something else. What was your question?"

"Is Banner an influence on you, his *Dr. Judge's Family* strip?"

"Soap opera," sneered a fan, "uck."

"Sure," answered Bert, "I suppose everybody's been influenced by Ty Banner's work. He's a damn good artist who—"

"Talking heads," said a fan. "Talking heads and buildings. The man's in a rut. Now take Texaco, who is obviously a disciple, his style is lively and—"

"I have to talk to you, Bert."

Carolyn Frame had pushed up to the table. Reaching out, she touched his arm.

"A foxy lady."

"Bet she isn't in comics."

"Too cute."

"Miss, miss, are you somebody? Sign my cup."

Frowning, Bert got up. "I'll be taking a short break now, gang," he announced.

The coffee shop attached to the convention motel was chill, the scents of hotcakes and bacon thick in the air.

Carolyn had stirred another packet of artificial sweetener into her coffee. "Your wife told me you'd come here, so I drove up."

On the other side of the booth Bert asked, "Something important?"

"I wanted to talk to you," the blonde young woman said. "About the police investigation of Dolph's death."

"Are they paying attention to Mrs. Tunney's accusations?"

"No, that's just it. They think she's wacky."

"Well, since she's been claiming you and I drowned her husband, it's good news they don't believe—"

"They don't believe *anyone* murdered Dolph."

Bert asked, "How do you know?"

"Sidney Lenzer told me when I phoned him this morning," replied Carolyn. "He's been able to find out what the police in Westport think."

"And they've concluded it's an accident?"

"Yes. They've finished their investigation and released his body for burial." She paused, began softly crying. "I can't even . . . go to his funeral."

100

"Funerals are never that much fun, so you're not missing anything."

She grabbed up her napkin from her lap, dabbed at her eyes, blew her nose. "I'm not in the mood for cheap remarks," she told him. "I loved Dolph . . . and . . . I was hoping to . . . to be able to attend his funeral."

"That would set off Mrs. Tunney."

"I know." Carolyn blew her nose once more. "I haven't heard from you in a couple of days. Have you given up?"

"No, I'm still looking into—"

"Seems to me a stupid comics convention in the middle of nowhere isn't a very choice spot to look for clues," she said, sniffling. "Or am I missing some important—"

"This I'm doing as a favor."

"To promote yourself."

"I don't work in comics anymore," he said, picking up his glass of orange juice.

"I'm being bitchy again," she decided. "Are you making, though, any progress?"

"Some."

"Can't you tell me?"

He said, "There are two or three possible reasons for what seems to be going on. The thing is, other people are involved."

"What people?"

"If I give you all the names, Carolyn, and then it turns out I'm on the wrong track . . . it might just make trouble."

"I won't tell anyone."

"Even so."

She asked, "Do you think there is a list? The way Dolph hinted?"

"One list at least, maybe two."

"Can't you please tell me the names?"

"Not yet."

"You're being asinine."

"Possibly."

She pushed away her untasted coffee. "If you don't have anything more to confide in me by the middle of this week, I'll start working on this alone."

"That's not too—"

"I'll phone you Wednesday." Sliding out of the booth, she went walking away.

# Chapter Sixteen

*B*ERT SAT GAZING out his living-room window at the night. The rain had ceased about an hour earlier. There was an open sketchbook resting on his knees, and he was doodling without much looking at the page.

"Bert?"

"Hum?"

His wife came into the room. "Can we talk about something that has nothing to do with comics, commercial art, or murder?"

"You have a specific topic in mind?" He noticed, as he started to close the sketchbook, that he'd been drawing a naked young woman walking into the surf.

"Me," Jan responded, sitting on the sofa opposite him.

"Are you okay? Is it a—"

"No, I'm in Grade A physical condition."

He fit the cap back on his pen. "Something wrong with the way things are going with our new house?"

"Nope." She shook her head. "What it is . . . well, I got a call from Boutiques, Inc. yesterday while you were out."

"And?"

"Tess Anderson . . . you met her, remember, at the Weston fireworks display two Fourth of Julys ago . . . Tess wanted to know if I'd be interested in doing some modeling for them again. For their print ads in local papers and magazines."

Bert said, "I thought you'd bid goodbye to all that."

"In a way I have. Except . . . the notion appeals to me now," she admitted. "It has been nearly three years since I sort of retired. See, Bert, I'm not talking about going into it full-time any more and having an agency in Manhattan represent me and all. But I thought it might be fun to work with Tess and maybe a few other local people. Money isn't fantastic, but it's money."

"Then go ahead," he said.

"Won't you feel threatened or abandoned?"

"Did I before?"

"That was the impression I had in the early days of our relationship."

He grinned. "Could be I have mellowed," he said. "It sounds fine to me."

"Good, then I'll call Tess in the morning." She crossed her legs, locked her hands around one knee. "You've been glum since you came home from the convention this afternoon. Was it depressing?"

"Not exactly. In fact, one kid told me I was nearly as good as Texaco."

"That should've buoyed you up," she said. "Did Carolyn's showing up there bother you?"

"Some, since she's threatening to start playing detective on her own," he answered. "Which can be unwise, as well as unsafe."

Jan watched him for a moment. "But there's something beyond that bothering you."

He left his chair. "I didn't give you a complete account of my interview with Mack Gruber when I came home yesterday."

"I sensed that."

From his shirt pocket he withdrew the notebook page Gruber had given him. Unfolding it, he handed it to his wife. "These are the six guys who raped Beverly Jepson."

"Gruber knew who . . . Oh, I see. Ty's on the list."

"Yeah."

"It happened twenty years ago, he was younger," Jan said. "Actually he doesn't strike me as the sort of man who'd ever do something like that."

"I don't think so either. But Gruber swears the—"

"What's Ty say?"

"We haven't talked about it yet."

"You better."

Nodding, he retrieved the list. "I'll phone him, see if I can drop over tonight."

Ty Banner's latest wife led Bert along the long hallway toward the studio. "Is my wig on cockeyed?"

"Is it a wig, Ellen?"

The tall, blonde Ellen Banner was forty-one and attractive. "Not tonight, no. But you've been looking at me oddly since I let you in."

"Fact is, I came across a picture of Martha O'Driscoll in a movie nostalgia book."

Ellen smiled. "Is she the one your fiery Latin friend says I resemble?"

"Yep, but I don't see it. You're much . . . sleeker."

"Thank you." She raised her hand to tap on the studio door. "Ty says you had an urgent reason for coming over tonight. I hope you and Jan aren't—"

"No, we have an idyllic marriage," he assured her. "This is something else."

"See if you can distract him from the drawing board. Ever since the strip started losing papers, he's been hustling outside work," she said. "Tonight it's a rush illustration job for *Golf Monthly*."

"Ty's a difficult man to—"

"Aha. Me wife and me trusted crony plotting against me behind my careworn back." Banner, clad in an ancient pair of slacks and a golf sweater, had flung open his door. He had a number-one watercolor brush over his ear.

"We'll work out the details later, Bert." Ellen patted him on the cheek and turned away. "But not that motel in Norwalk this time."

Banner raised his eyebrows. "Abe, I have to . . . but you," he said. "Remember that old joke? Harry Hershfield used to tell that at the Cartoonists Society dinners all the time. C'mon in, my boy."

When the door was shut on the large, orderly studio, Bert said, "We've known each other quite a while—"

"You in need of money? I think, without consulting the memsahib, we can let you have a thousand or maybe even—"

"No, my marriage is fine and I'm not in hock. Not enough to need a loan, anyway."

Banner returned to his drawing board. After sitting, he readjusted the gooseneck lamp. "I'm on pins and needles, old buddy. What is the problem?"

"Yesterday I had a talk with Mack Gruber."

"How is he?"

"Seems fine." Bert took the list from his pocket.

"What's that?"

"Gruber knows about the rape," said Bert carefully. "He wrote down the names of the six guys involved, as they were told to him. That was some time afterwards."

Banner asked, "Then Mack wasn't one of them?"

"Nope." Bert walked over to the board, thrust the list under the lamp's spill of light. "But he says you were."

Taking the slip of paper, Banner read it. "He's wrong," he said. "I'm not sure I was even at that particular party."

"I figured it was a mistake."

"But you aren't quite sure?" He let the list fall to his board.

"Well, I thought you ought to know about it."

Banner said, "Hibbard brought this whole lousy business up at that rap session I missed. He obviously was one of the six, and he knows who the others are."

"Gruber claims Hibbard's the one who filled him in on what took place," he told his friend. "But that was a year or so later, and they were both somewhat drunk."

"Hibbard was always drunk in those days. It's maybe pickled his brains," said Banner. "But I think if we jog the bastard's memory, he'll recall who really took part."

"We'd better talk to Hibbard."

"Do you think he mentioned my name at the session?" Banner was on his feet. "A couple of the fellows, now I think on it, did eye me rather oddly when next I attended."

"Want to phone Hibbard, see if—"

"That I do, my boy." He crossed to the file cabinet with the telephone atop it. "He resides in your hometown of Brimstone." After consulting an address wheel, Banner punched out a number. "He's got to amend this bloody list so my . . . Hello, Fred? What?"

Bert moved closer, sensing something was wrong.

"This is Ty Banner," Banner was saying. "I'm a friend of Fred's and . . . who am I talking to? Is Betty around . . . Detective Furtado? What's going . . . I see. Yes, I see. When?" He clapped his hand over the mouthpiece. "Fred fell from the deck outside his studio, broke his neck on the patio below. His wife found him when she got back from shopping at—"

"Let me talk to Furtado."

Banner handed him the phone.

"Detective Furtado," said Bert. "This is Bert Kurrie."

"I'm in the middle of a—"

"You're in the middle of a series of murders," Bert said. "Beau Jassminsky was number two and Hibbard's number four. There could be at least two more."

"What we have here, Kurrie, is an accident."

"Four accidents in less than two weeks? C'mon, that's impossible," he said. "Not when all four men are linked together closely."

"They are? That comes as news to me." The policeman's

voice was slightly nasal. "Fact is, I don't even know what the hell four men we're talking about, so—"

"We ought to discuss this."

There were several seconds of silence. Then Detective Furtado said, "Meet me in two hours at the Brimstone Police Station. Can you?"

"Sure."

"You know where the—"

"Right across from the recycling lot."

"That's the place," said Furtado. "See you then."

# Chapter Seventeen

"ALLERGIES," EXPLAINED Detective Furtado as he plucked another tissue from the box on his desk and wiped his nose. "I used to think what I had was hay fever, but then my wife got me to go to a specialist, and it turns out I suffer from multiple allergies." He crumpled the paper handkerchief, dropped it in his yellow plastic wastebasket.

"Can't you take something for that?" inquired Bert.

"They wanted to give me shots, but I don't like that idea. This only hits me hard about two, three weeks every spring." Furtado was a short, thickset man of thirty-nine. Dark, his hair thinning. "Antihistamines make me woozy." Taking another tissue, he blew his nose. "You think we ought to be looking for a mad killer, huh?"

The policeman's office was small, with pale green walls and one little window looking out on a stretch of parking lot.

Bert was sitting in a metal-and-plastic chair. "I've got some names here."

Furtado took the list, scanned it. "Three of these guys are dead."

"Four," corrected Bert. "Leon Brenner died a couple weeks back, over in Westchester County."

"How?"

"Supposedly in his sleep, after a long illness."

Setting the list aside, Furtado grabbed another tissue. "Where'd you get these names?"

"From Mack Gruber. He lives in Westport," Bert answered. "The thing is, I got the list yesterday."

Furtado's left eye narrowed. "How'd Gruber know Hibbard was going to die?"

"He didn't . . . or maybe he did."

"Which?"

"Okay, let me backtrack and explain what may be going on," said Bert. "Oh, and I don't think Ty Banner's name belongs with those others."

Furtado blew his nose once again.

Bert continued, "All the guys on the list worked in Manhattan for an outfit called Kreative Komics. This was twenty-some years ago. The company is still going strong, but none—"

"I know about KK. My thirteen-year-old son's a comics nut. Even drags me to comics conventions now and again. Fact is, there was one up in New Haven today, but I couldn't—"

"You missed seeing me in action. Anyway, all six men worked at Kreative. The company, more or less legally, stole Gruber's Captain Thunderbolt from him."

"Yeah, he's the guy used to draw that. Recently released from a rest home."

"It could be Gruber has a grudge against certain people and is—"

"He's being damn helpful if he's the killer, Kurrie, giving you an advance list of his victims."

"A good way to divert suspicion."

"In comic books, maybe."

"Gruber wrote a lot of them," Bert said. "There's something else, though, that these men have in common. Except for Ty Banner, they all took part in the gang rape of a young woman who worked at KK."

"When was this?" He straightened up in his chair.

"Back twenty years ago. The girl was from Westport, named Beverly Jepson, and she—"

"Killed herself by walking into the ocean," the policeman said. "Yeah, I remember that. I was in college at UB then."

"Hibbard brought up that incident at a rap group recently," Bert went on. "They were talking about guilt and this was, obviously, something Hibbard felt guilty about. He talked about the rape, gave out the names of all the others involved."

"Is Gruber in this amateur-therapy bunch?"

"No, he says Hibbard told him about the rape years ago and he's kept the names in mind ever since," answered Bert. "Hibbard was apparently something of a lush and . . . well, Ty says he didn't take part and I believe him."

Tapping the slip of paper, Furtado asked, "Do the names he gave out at the rap session match these?"

"Not sure."

"Who else is in the group?"

"Ty Banner is, but he missed that session. Warren Snyder, a professor at UB. I've talked to him and he doesn't remember all the names mentioned, since he didn't know most of the men," said Bert. "I don't know any of the other members, but Ty could tell you."

Furtado brushed at his nose with a fresh white tissue. "Suppose somebody decided to knock off all the gents who raped Beverly Jepson," he said slowly, "who is he and what's his motive?"

"Has to be someone who was close to her, one way or the other. Right now I don't know if any of her family is still around."

"Say it's her dear old dad, her kid brother or even her old college sweetheart," said the policeman. "Or maybe even one of the rapists who's gone bonkers with remorse. Why's the wait so long for his revenge?"

"If somebody just went crazy, that would explain it,"

said Bert. "Could be, though, that he just learned the names or that he's been away and couldn't do anything until now."

"Been away in some place like a rest home?"

"There's also prison, the service. I don't know." Bert scratched at his ribs. "It's also occurred to me, although I admit this is sort of farfetched, that Beverly Jepson might not be dead."

"She fakes her suicide, runs away and starts a new life under a new name?"

"People have done things like that."

"So twenty long years later, she returns to her old hometown and decides to start killing off these louts."

"They never found her body," said Bert. "Everyone tends to think of her the way she looked then, a pretty brunette in her twenties. She could be fat and gray now, or skinny and dyed blonde."

"Or moldering at the bottom of the Sound someplace."

"Sure, that's the most likely possibility, but . . . ."

"You used to work in comics, too."

"At Maximus."

"You have a pretty good imagination."

"You mean you don't believe there's—"

"Three men, make that four men, can die as the result of fatal accidents in a short period of time," the police detective said, wiping at his nose. "Read the obits every day and you'll see that's not odd. But when all four appear to have several things in common, that sounds like something else again. Kurrie, I'm going to think about this and talk to some people."

"The killer's moving fast, so there's not that much time for—"

"I know where Ty Banner is. What about Marvin Appel?"

"Not certain. Ty thinks he may be living over in Westchester someplace, working as an assistant to a newspaper cartoonist," Bert replied. "I'm going to try to track him down."

"I can handle that better."

"You're telling me I can't?"

Furtado shook his head. "Do what you will," he said. "But do try, Kurrie, not to have a fatal accident yourself."


"Mind if I nag?"

Bert pushed back from his drawing board. "Commence," he invited.

His wife, wearing a terry robe, came into the studio. "It's nigh on to one A.M."

"Couldn't sleep."

"You working?"

"On that *Swordmaiden* cover. Roughs."

"Back when you were slaving for Maximus Comics, and they dumped all those impossible deadlines on you, you stayed up late too many nights."

"I'm not," he assured her, "falling back on my old low-down ways."

"I strive to be supportive."

"You're a brick. Heard somebody say that on the late show once."

"I want you to understand that the rational part of me is proud of you, of your dedication to trying to solve these killings and stop any more from happening." She rubbed her knuckle across a spot just below her breasts. "Inside, though, I really am starting to get scared."

"I don't believe I'm in danger, not much anyway."

"Every time you go out to talk to someone about this mess, you come home and report the guy's dead and gone," Jan said, still rubbing at her chest. "You're tracking someone who's goofy, so you can't predict that—"

"This killer isn't necessarily nuts. There could be a fairly sensible, to him, motive for—"

"I'm not talking legal definitions of sanity and insanity," she said. "What I mean is . . . look, here's someone who shoved Beau Jassminsky off a cliff, drowned Tunney, and then threw that other man . . . Hibbard . . . off his deck. He probably even smothered the first one or did something equally nasty to him."

"He's out to get a specific group of people."

"You can darn well bet that if you get in his way, he's going to hurt you, too," she said. "I really wouldn't like to come home and find you dead in the bathtub or sprawled on the—"

"Easy, easy." He went over, sat beside her, and put an arm around her shoulders. "He'll try for the two left on the list before he—"

"Has it occurred to you that you may have the wrong list?"

"Hum?"

"The names Gruber provided are the people who may, or may not, have raped the Jepson girl," Jan said. "You don't have any guarantee the killer's going by the same list. Maybe he's after ten people or two dozen."

"Granted, but four names on my list are right. It figures at least—"

"He's going to try to kill you, too."

"Nope, I'll make sure that doesn't happen."

"Tunney supposedly knew something, that there was a list and that he was on it," she reminded. "Okay, but he was killed anyway."

"Probably because the murderer was someone he knew or someone he thought he could trust," he said. "Me, I'm going to be suspicious of anyone who so much as—"

"All right, okay," Jan said, sighing slightly. "I see I can't dissuade you."

"That's a nifty word. Dissuade."

"It seemed apt," she said. "Can I help you on this, then?"

"And get hurt, too?"

114

"Well, heck, we might as well sink into oblivion to-gether."

"Tomorrow . . . today I guess it is by now . . . I want to see if I can locate Marvin Appel."

"The other survivor besides Ty."

"Ty has the notion Appel's been assisting Al Truett on the *Race Sentry* newspaper strip," Bert said. "I'll check that out. You might see if you can discover what happened to Beverly Jepson's parents and relations."

"That sounds relatively tame."

"Let us hope so."

# Chapter Eighteen

Bᴇʀᴛ ᴡᴀs ʀᴇᴀᴄʜɪɴɢ for his studio phone when Jan appeared in the doorway. "The tour of famous artists' studios has been postponed, ma'am," he said. "However, if you'd like to pop in and fool around with one famous artist, long as you're here, why—"

"Sounds like it might be great fun, but I'm en route to the Westport town hall," his wife informed him, "to see if I can find out what's become of the Jepson family. Did you know their town hall is on Myrtle Street?"

"Posh towns have posh street names like that," he said. "If I can set up a meeting with Appel, I'll leave you a note."

"Be cautious, okay?"

Going over, he kissed her. "You, too."

Smiling, she departed.

Bert returned to the phone and dialed Al Truett's number.

On the fourth ring, a young woman answered. "Alfred Truett studio."

"Al there?"

"Whom shall I say is calling?"

"Bert Kurrie."

The young woman inquired, "Is Mr. Truett acquainted with you?"

"We know each other somewhat. From Newspaper Artist Guild meetings and such. Ty Banner will vouch for me."

"Is Mr. Truett acquainted with Mr. Banner?"

"They're old golfing buddies."

"Hold on."

Picking up a pencil, Bert doodled on the message pad. A sketch of a young woman sitting on a cake of ice.

"Bert? How are you?"

"I'm glad you decided you were acquainted with me."

Truett chuckled. "Alicia's new, only been with us six weeks."

"*Race Sentry*'s still looking good, Al."

"What paper do you follow it in?"

Bert struggled to recall where he'd last noticed the adventure strip back several months ago. "The . . . Norwalk *Hour*."

"We've had that darn paper since the strip started in 1949. They love me in Norwalk."

"One hears that on the streets frequently. 'We love Truett,' and similar chants."

Chuckling again, the cartoonist said, "*Race* still runs in 650 papers, damn good for a straight continuity strip these days. Especially for one about a career marine. I hear Ty's losing papers."

"One or two small ones."

"If he can call the Detroit *News* small, he's in better shape than I thought. Now what can I do for you, Bert?"

"Actually, I'm trying to get hold of Marvin Appel. He's your assistant, isn't he?"

There was a short silence over in Westchester. Then Truett asked, "Why do you want Marv?"

"Well, it's somewhat complicated," Bert said. "There've been a few deaths of artists and cartoonists here in Fairfield in the past few—"

"I heard about Beau. Who else?"

"Dolph Tunney and Fred Hibbard."

"I figured Hibbard would've drunk himself to death long before this. What happened to him?"

"The police think," said Bert, embellishing the truth a bit, "all of them may have been murdered."

Another spell of silence. "What's Marv got to do with any of this?"

"Could be nothing, but he used to work with all these guys, and I'm anxious to talk to him."

"I'm sixty-six years old, you know."

"I didn't."

"I'm in damn good shape and I take care of myself. I'm amazed, though, at the number of my colleagues who don't, at the number who are drunks."

"Hibbard, you mean?"

"Hibbard and Marv Appel," answered Truett. "To me, there are enough pressures in this damn business without adding booze."

Bert asked, "Appel doesn't work for you anymore?"

"Not for eight months, no. He was with me on *Race* for eleven years and he wasn't bad," said the cartoonist. "He was a good letterer, hell of a lot better than I am. About a year ago he started to go to pieces. I kept him on longer than I should have, mostly because of his wife. Did you know Sally Appel?"

"No."

"She died of cancer, year ago. Marv'd always been a drinker, but that pushed him over," he said. "He got so bad at times that neighbors had to call the police emergency ambulance to revive the poor bastard. I carried him as long as I could, then just had to get someone new. You don't hold 650 papers with fuzzy lettering and hazy backgrounds."

"Do you know where he is now?"

"It's really important to you to talk to him?"

"I think so, yes."

"All right, but I'd prefer you don't tell him I gave you this information," said Truett. "I've helped Marv a few times since he left me and then I had to quit that, too. He got to be a pest about money, and I'm not set up to be a social welfare agency. I know, I make a hell of a lot of money from *Race*. I wasn't put on Earth to finance winos and deadbeats."

"I won't mention you at all."

"Actually he's over in Connecticut, not too far from where you are," said Truett. "Bridgeport isn't too far from you, is it?"

"Twenty minutes or so. He's living in Bridgeport?"

"If you can call it living. He has a brother or cousin there, and he lived with him for a while. But they couldn't put up with him, tossed him on his can."

"Where is he now?"

"The place is called the Maple Hotel. It's on the edge of the tenderloin, inhabited by pensioners and broken-down old farts. Marv's only fifty-six, yet he seems to be living the life of a senior citizen."

"Maple Hotel." He wrote the name under a doodle.

"Let me warn you, he'll hit you for money."

"I may give him some, if it'll help to get him talking."

"Give him money once," advised Truett. "Don't let him know where he can find you. Otherwise he'll hound you, phone you and whine for handouts. It's a shame really, since Marv had a lot of potential. Anything else or can I get back to the board?"

"Nope, and thanks."

Bert hung up and was about to pick up the phone again to dial Bridgeport information.

The phone rang.

"Hello."

"What the hell is going on?"

"Be more specific, Carolyn."

"Fred Hibbard. The story just came into the paper. He worked at Kreative Komics, too. I remember Dolph mentioning him."

"Hibbard died last night in a fall. It looked like an accident."

"Jesus, how many people are going to—"

"Look, I'm trying to get hold of somebody in connection with this," Bert told her. "It could lead someplace and I'll phone you soon as—"

"What about the damn police? Do they still maintain these things are accidents?"

"Not sure. I talked to Detective Furtado last night and—"

"Did he listen to you, does he believe you?"

"He didn't toss me out. I have the feeling he believed at least some of what I told him."

"How about that asshole Sergeant Swanson of the Westport cops? You'll need a dozen eyewitnesses, videotape instant replays and the voice of God to convince him Dolph was murdered."

"Furtado's going to talk to Swanson, I'm sure. So they—"

"It's very difficult for me to relax, Bert, and wait around calmly."

"Once I know something I'll—"

"I have to know who killed Dolph."

"That's what I'm trying to—"

"Hell, they're giving me the fish eye here in Want Ads. Talk to you later."

"Bye." He cradled the receiver.

The phone rang again.

"Hello already."

"Ah, it's a relief to hear your surly snarl, effendi."

"Hi, Texaco."

"I'm ensconced here in my crib at Maximus Comics, Inc., whipping out a rush KnightOwl job," said Texaco from Manhattan. "When I reached the panel wherein our hero disembowels six espionage agents from Parallel Universe Russia with naught but the special stilettos built into his special platinum gloves, I decided it was time to take a small break."

"Sounds like a fine place to halt."

"Well, I may have to trot over to the public library for some medical books. Carlotsky is a stickler for authenticity and I want to get all these Russian innards right."

"Parallel Universe Russian innards. Can't you fake those?"

"I'm hoping I have some useful scrap in my own swipe files, but thus far I'm too timid to look into my intestines and other inside parts file," the cartoonist said. "And now, sir, to the real purpose of this electronic intrusion. I was just chatting with my other sahib, the venerable Ty Banner."

"That probably did more for you than calling Dial-A-Prayer."

"Sad to say, amigo, it didn't. Fact, it caused a pall of gloom to settle over my manly locks. You remember Manly Locks, Goldie's brother? But seriously, Ty informs me that yet another Kreative Komics alum has bit the dust."

"Last night, yeah. Fred Hibbard."

"Ty further states that you are up to your teakettle in this mess still. You were hobnobbing with the local minions of the law out there instead of jumping in bed and pulling the covers over your head. Both the Surgeon General and I conclude that messing with this any longer, Bert, will be dangerous to your health."

"I'm okay. Nobody's going to arrange an accident for me or—"

"Famous last words."

"Really, I can handle—"

"Suppose I scoot out there? Maybe I can even camp in your living room for a few—"

"You can't leave KnightOwl in the lurch. You're a pro, Texaco, and the work comes—"

"But you, amigo, ought not to be prowling around alone."

"I appreciate your concern, but I don't need a body-guard."

"I know I'm small, but I'm cunning. Years of street fighting in my younger days has made me—"

"Listen, I've got to locate somebody in Bridgeport. I'll call you tonight. Okay?"

"You drew superheroes up here too long," warned Texaco, "and now you're starting to think you're one yourself. Beware."

# Chapter Nineteen

*T*HERE WAS NOTHING next door to the Maple Hotel except a weedy field and a cracked cement stairway that must've belonged to the building that had stood there years before. The hotel was on a corner, a six-story stone building the dark orangish color of rotten apples.

Bert parked his car across the street beside another weedy lot. This one was surrounded by a hurricane fence, and sprawled across it were mounds of old bottles, a few blown-out truck tires, and the rusty skeleton of a bicycle.

On the steps of a skinny green apartment house, two old men sat staring at nothing.

Crossing the street, Bert entered the lobby of the hotel. It was a fairly large lobby, dotted with ancient couches and armchairs, smelling strongly of must and disinfectant.

There was no one in any of the chairs, although a battered black-and-white television set was giving the midday news atop a lame table.

The clerk was a fat man of forty, clad in denim shirt and khaki trousers. He'd been tattooed some time before he put on weight, and the green snakes and crimson hearts and daggers that decorated his plump lower arms were distorted and blurred. "Yes, sir?"

"I phoned you about Marvin Appel."

"He still isn't in."

Bert asked, "Any idea where he might be?"

"You a relative?"

"A friend of his asked me to look him up."

"You got some money for him?"

"I might."

The clerk scratched his chin. The flower tattooed on the back of his hand seemed about to explode. "Was he really a big-time cartoonist once?"

"Pretty much so."

"Did he ever really draw *Race Sentry?*"

"For eleven years."

"You hear a lot of bullshit around here. Never know who to believe."

"Would he be at a bar?"

"He most always is."

"Any particular one?"

"I'd try the Sawdust Trail first. Around the corner next to the barbershop," said the clerk with a point to the right. "Can't miss the shop because they got a lady barber works there. A platinum blonde one that weighs over three hundred pounds."

"I'll take a look as I pass."

"She's a dyke, but a damn good barber."

Nodding, Bert said, "Thanks."

A third old man, wrapped in a faded blue overcoat, had joined the others across the way. He was staring, too.

The barbershop had an Out To Lunch sign dangling in the window, so he didn't get to see the formidable lady barber.

The Sawdust Trail had authentic looking Old West saloon swinging doors. There were at least a half dozen moose and elk heads mounted up on the knotty pine walls. Mixed with the odors of stale beer and neglected bathrooms was the scent of the same disinfectant the hotel went in for. A bar ran along one wall of the narrow room, booths along the other. The booths were empty, but seven men, mostly old and gray, hunched along the bar on the spindly-legged stools. The bartender was a black man with rimless glasses and a polka-dot bow tie.

Bert surveyed the customers from a spot just over the threshold. Only one appeared young enough to be Appel. He'd taken a look at the cartoonist's photo in the old Kreative Komics promotion booklet, but didn't expect him to look much like that any longer.

"Yes, sir?" asked the bartender.

Walking over to the bar, Bert halted near the man who might be Appel. "I'm looking for Marv Appel."

The bartender asked, "How come?"

"A friend of his, Al Truett, told me I might find him around here, so—"

"I'm Appel," said the thin, sandy-haired man next to him.

"My name's Bert Kurrie. I'd like to talk to you."

None of Appel's clothes quite fit. His blue windbreaker was three sizes too large, his denim slacks were too tight, the tail of his plaid flannel shirt hung out. There was a smudge of beard on his gaunt face, too many wrinkles and the scabs of several cuts. "What about?"

"Your days with Kreative Komics, some of the people you knew."

Appel drank from his glass of beer, then from his shot glass of whiskey. "You a historian?"

"Nope, just a commercial artist. What I'm trying to find out about is—"

"I'm an artist, too. No longer commercial."

"Al Truett told me—"

"Screw dear old Alfred Truett," said the cartoonist. "I imagine he told you not to loan me any money since I'd only drink it up."

"Matter of fact, he did. But that—"

"And he no doubt gave you a speech about what great potential I once had."

Nodding, Bert said nothing.

"Well, that's a lot of crap. I've been second-rate all my life." Appel paused to drink from each glass in turn. "Only a second-rate jerk would end up giving eleven frigging years of his life to pencilling *Race Sentry* and lettering it. Do you know what Truett earns a year?"

"Around two hundred thousand."

"Three hundred and fifty thousand. A guaranteed hundred thousand from the strip and the rest from merchandising. Books, toys, reprints, premiums. And it's the dumbest strip I ever laid eyes on. Jesus, a hero who's been a marine for thirty years."

"What I'm interested in is the time you were at KK."

"Why?"

"Things have been happening to some of the people who were there in the 1960s and—"

"Death," cut in Appel. "That's what's been happening. I read about . . . what the hell was his name, that big husky oaf? Beau Jassminsky. I read all about him in the Bridgeport *Post*. Also about Dolph Tunney. Maybe they're better off. Do you know what Truett paid me to work on his nitwit strip?"

"Not enough."

"Damn right. Two hundred dollars a week. That's eight hundred dollars a month, and he was making over a quarter million."

"Could we talk over in a booth?"

"Can you loan me some money?"

"Sure."

"Let's see it."

Bert got a twenty out of his wallet. "Here."

"A deal." Appel's knobby hand snatched the bill. "Jess, another round for me. What are you drinking?"

"Nothing."

"Don't drink?"

"Not anymore."

"Smart." Appel, a little wobbly in the legs, carried his beer and his shot to a shadowy booth. "You married?"

"Yes."

"I was." He stumbled, almost spilling the beer, as he settled into the green-painted wooden booth. "My wife died."

"Yes, I heard."

"Cancer. Quick. Three months and she was gone," he said. "People told me that was for the best. She didn't suffer long. That, though, is a lot of bullshit. The only good thing is to be alive. And she isn't anymore." He drank some of the beer, some of the whiskey. "What do you want to know?"

"You remember Beverly Jepson?"

Appel looked up from his drinks, watching Bert's face with his watery eyes. "Is that what's catching up with those guys?"

"Might be. Were you one of them?"

"Jesus, that must've happened . . . help me . . . fifteen years ago?"

"Twenty."

"Twenty. I was no kid, should've known better." He leaned back into the shadows. "Hell, if I'd been able to control myself when I drank I wouldn't have ended up here. Right? Five of us did it."

"Five? Only five."

"That's more than enough for a gang bang, believe me."

"You remember who?"

Appel touched at the pockets of his windbreaker. "Did you already give me that twenty?"

"Yep."

"Where the hell'd I put it?"

"Your hip pocket."

Appel raised up, felt at his backside. "Yeah, it's there. What were you asking me?"

"The names of those five guys."

"She was really pretty. Aloof, though, and never too friendly to most of us. But I think maybe she was different with the other guy, but you never know."

"What other guy?"

"I'm not sure who he was. But one time . . . we used to clown around up there at KK quite a lot . . . one time I spotted her looking at something she kept in her top desk drawer. I snuck up and grabbed it."

"A photo?"

"Right, of a good-looking guy. Bev snatched it back before I got a very good look." Appel's eyes were nearly closed as he leaned back and remembered. "Next day I waited until she was out to lunch and opened the drawer. Picture was gone."

"You never asked her who it was?"

"She wasn't the kind of girl you asked questions like that."

Bert said, "Can you give me the names of the five men?"

From his jacket pocket Appel took a ballpoint pen. "I'll write them for you." He pulled a napkin free of the table dispenser. "I'm one of the best letterers in the business. I lettered Captain Thunderbolt for years, up until I went to work for bighearted Alfie Truett."

"Have you seen Mack Gruber lately?" Bert tried not to watch the cartoonist's shaking hand.

"Not for years. They put the poor bastard away somewhere, I heard."

"He's out now, living in Westport."

"I bet with that rich sister." Appel crossed out a letter, began again on the second name. "Whether you're rich or poor, it helps to have money. Old Chinese proverb."

"You have a brother in Bridgeport?"

"A first cousin. Can't blame him for wanting me out.

Most of the time I don't even like being around me." Appel hunched his narrow shoulders, concentrating on his list. "Stupidest thing most of us ever did, what we did to Bev. When I took a few drinks, I was never too smart." He clicked his pen; the tip retracted. "There you go."

The lettering on the napkin was shaky, some of the letters were reversed. It was the way you lettered in comics and movies when you wanted to show a kid had made the sign. L∃MONAD∃ FUR SAL∃ and so on. "You're sure there were just five?"

"Hell, five was more than enough."

The names Appel had put down were Marv Appel, Fred Hibbard, Leon Brenner, Beau Jassminsky, Dolph Tunney.

After folding the napkin, Bert put it in his shirt pocket. "Ty Banner wasn't with you?"

"Ty? Hell, no."

"Hibbard told somebody Ty was."

"Hibbard, most times, couldn't remember his own name, let alone anybody else's," said Appel. "No, Ty . . . I don't think he was even at that damn party. You know, though . . . what did you say your name was?"

"Bert Kurrie."

"Bert, I remember Fred saying something about, 'It's too bad Ty's not here. He's always had the idea Bev thinks he's just terrific.' I told him Ty wouldn't want to join in anyway. He was a loner. Maybe, after a while, Fred couldn't exactly remember if Ty'd been in on that mess or not. Did you say you were an artist?"

"I do paperback covers. Used to be at Maximus."

Appel laughed. "Carlotsky still up there?"

"Afraid so."

"You know, Bert, there are a lot of mean bastards in comics, but Carlotsky is the champ. I did a couple books for him years ago on *The Five Avengers*, and the son of a bitch made his suggested corrections right on my finished art in grease pencil. Hell, meant I had to draw those damn pages all over from scratch."

"That's Carlotsky." Bert glanced around the afternoon barroom. "Listen, I think somebody is out to kill some of the guys who worked at KK."

"Why'd anybody do that? Because of Bev, you mean?"

"That might be the reason, I'm not sure. The list you just did for me . . . you're the only one on it who's still alive."

"No shit?" After laughing, Appel drank at his beer. "And I'm not all that alive myself."

"This cousin of yours, could you move back with him until—"

"It wasn't just my cousin who gave me the heave-ho. His wife, a true-blue bitch, was the mastermind behind that." He shook his head. "No way I could go there again."

"Do you have some other—"

"A son in California, big executive in Silicon Valley," he said. "He doesn't want me either. No, he never much liked me even when I was sober. When Sally died . . . when my wife died, he didn't even come back for the funeral."

Bert said, "You ought to have someone keeping an eye on you."

"Naw, I'm okay. You don't have to—"

"Somebody may try to kill you."

Appel shrugged. "To tell you the truth . . . Bert, isn't it? To tell you the truth, Bert, I don't much care."

"At least be careful," he cautioned, without much hope it would do any good. "Don't go anywhere at night for a while, don't—"

"I never much go anywhere but Harpoon Louie's down the block or here." He drank his shot of whiskey. "Long as I have a little money, there's no need to go anywhere else."

Bert gave him another ten. "Thanks for talking to me."

"Sure you don't want a drink?"

Shaking his head, Bert eased out of the green booth.

He went back into the Maple Hotel lobby to use the phone booth. He'd call Detective Furtado and tell him about finding Marvin Appel. He knew, though, that nobody was going to bother to protect him.

# Chapter Twenty

$T$UESDAY MORNING THE 11:05 train got into the Westport station at 11:16.

Bert was waiting down in the large parking lot, watching the ramps that led down from the train platform.

Texaco emerged from the last car, in the wake of a slim blonde. He spotted Bert, waved, pointed at the young woman's back.

"Did you notice that?" the curlyhaired cartoonist asked while he and Bert were shaking hands.

"Pretty blonde, on the skinny side."

"Sahib, she was an exact replica of Louise Allbritton in her prime."

"Oh, sure, everyone in Westport has noticed that. We take it for granted."

"She isn't from Westport, amigo. The fetching lass resides in Yonkers, of all places, and is visiting this fair town to spend a day with her maiden aunt who . . . Santa Maria! There she goes, climbing into that Mercedes 220S piloted by that sun-browned oaf in tennis togs."

"Probably the aunt's live-in love." He started guiding his friend to the spot in the ten-minute zone where he'd left his car. "You conversed with her en route?"

"We are all but travelers on the road to oblivion, my son, and so we ought to converse with whomsoever we meet along the route of the journey," replied Texaco, climbing into the passenger seat. "Especially with fellow travelers who look like slim 1940s movie ladies."

Hooking up his seat belt, Bert asked, "You're sure Carlotsky doesn't mind your taking the day off?"

"Due to my incredible dexterity and fabled swiftness, I finished that nineteen-page KnightOwl yarn ahead of schedule. Disembowelments, impalings and all."

"Okay, fine. But I still don't really need a guardian angel or—"

"Isn't it really because I'm a despicable Latino and not worthy to touch the hem of the average Westport WASP that you don't want me hanging around?"

"That, too." Bert started the car, maneuvered it through the mixture of disembarked passengers and departing autos. "But, as I mentioned when you phoned last night, I appreciate your offer to tag along today. Probably won't turn out too exciting."

"Any news of Appel, is the lad still extant?"

"I called the Maple Hotel this morning, and they tell me he's at his usual spot in the Sawdust Trail bar," he answered. "Detective Furtado, of our Brimstone police, promised he'd talk to the Bridgeport cops about Appel."

"They aren't likely to expend too much effort on a tenderloin wino."

"Nope." They drove across the small bridge that spanned the Saugatuck River.

"Have you thought about staking the chap out yourself? I hear they catch lots of tigers in India by tying a goat to a stake."

"Watch Appel until somebody comes to kill him? That's a possibility, except the killer may also have Ty on his list."

"What's Ty say about all this?"

"He just doesn't believe anyone can be out to get him."

136

He turned onto Compo Road. "He probably considers me demented and misguided."

"I have faith in you," Texaco assured him. "You're foolhardy, but not goofy. How about, then, keeping an eye on my sometime lord and master? Instead of Appel."

"We don't know which one the killer'll go for first. Be much better to find him before he makes a try for either."

"I forget. How does one go about doing that?"

"Well, I've been thinking that this old boyfriend of Beverly Jepson's, the one Appel saw the picture of once, might be somebody to talk to."

"He might be somebody with a motive for knocking off the fellers who raped her."

"Jan found out yesterday that both Beverly Jepson's parents are dead," said Bert. "There are no close relatives in this area, and their house was inherited by the husband's brother out in Muscatine, Iowa."

"Sounds like a dead end then, Inspector."

"Except for the fact that no one's lived in their Westport house since the father died three and a half years ago," he said. "The place needed quite a few repairs, and the brother apparently decided to let them slide until he came back here and lived in the house. He hasn't done that yet—may never, the real estate folks think. So he pays the property taxes and the place sits."

"You're counting on artifacts and papers having been left in the joint?"

"Far as we've been able to tell, nothing was sent to the brother," said Bert. "It all depends on what was saved. Jan's tracked down the real estate office that looks after the house. We're going to meet her there."

"She'll be able to persuade them to let us in to poke around?"

"If Jan can't, we'll give them a dose of your sultry charm."

Texaco locked his hands behind his head. "Come what may, bwana," he said, "it'll beat spending the day under the same roof with Carlotsky."

There was an iron gate in the high white stone wall that surrounded the Jepson property. It was held shut with a loop of rusted iron and a heavy padlock.

Bert braked a few feet short of the gate. "She give you a key for this?"

"Mrs. Tinkelman of Nutmeg Square Realty provided me with a key for every purpose." His wife dug into her purse and produced a large brass key with a red tag attached. "Front gate."

Reaching over from the back seat, Texaco took the key from her hand. "Allow me." Stepping out of the idling car, he went trotting toward the gate. "Good thing it's still broad daylight."

"He's really concerned about you," said Jan, watching Texaco fiddle with the lock.

"Much like you, he thinks I'm not qualified to look after myself."

"Everybody can use a couple of stalwart sidekicks. Juan and I are sort of what Robin is to Batman, what Butch Cassidy—"

"What Larry and Curly are to Moe."

"*Voila!*" exclaimed Texaco, shoving the unlocked gate open. The hinges shrieked.

Bert put the car in gear and rolled onto the two and a half acres that stretched beyond the gateway. "Cheery," he observed.

The curving gravel drive, splotched with clumps of spiky weeds, twisted through a lawn that was now high grass and tall flowering weeds. There were maple trees, willows, and birches dotting the grounds. One of the trees had died, and its heaviest branch hung down, cracked nearly free of the trunk and dangling.

Texaco jogged along beside the slow-moving car. "A perfect place for Evelyn Ankers."

"Who's Evelyn Ankers?" Jan asked her husband.

"A 1940s movie actress."

"You sure?"

"Every woman he alludes to is a 1940s actress."

The house was a large three-story Victorian. It was a pale gold in color, the intricate gingerbread trim a muddy white. Shutters masked the ground-floor windows.

Bert parked near the wide wooden front steps. "Dredge up the front-door key."

She pressed a silver key into his palm. "I think Mrs. Tinkelman is still a mite unclear about what we're up to."

"The impression I got from listening to you was that we were either going to try to buy this place from the heir or use it in part of a complicated genealogical study."

"Hooey. I was quite straightforward." She got out of the car.

Texaco was already on the top step of the porch. "I usually carry a handful of werewolf food in my pocket, but wouldn't you know, today I clean forgot."

"This place isn't spooky," Jan told him as she climbed the stairs. "In fact, it's sort of charming."

"Some people thought Hitler was sort of charming," the little cartoonist said. "No, in matters of this sort you have to trust a primitive type like me, Jan. I maintain the joint is haunted."

Bert tried the key in the lock. "Some bodyguard," he said.

"I see myself in the Mantan Moreland role," he said. "A bodyguard up to a point, and then I'm going to roll my eyes and holler, 'Feets, do your stuff!' "

"Damn, this thing's sticking." Bert gave the key a few more twists and finally managed to unlock the door. He turned the brass knob, pushed and the heavy oaken door creaked open.

"True to form," remarked Texaco. "Haunted house, creaking door."

The smell of emptiness hung heavy in the air of the long, shadowy hallway.

Bert walked along the dusty carpeting, glancing around. "Nobody's been here for a long time."

"Maybe they know something we don't." Texaco paused to study himself in the dust-smeared mirror in the hall on his left.

"Bedrooms are probably upstairs," said Bert. "I'll see if I can find Beverly's. It's possible they left some of her stuff there after she died. Jan, maybe you can look for a den or study down on this floor where they kept family papers and such."

Nodding, Jan clicked a wall switch. A large overhead globe of light came on. "They keep the electricity on."

"Good," said Texaco. "You can't have too much light in a mausoleum like this."

"You want to see what's in the cellar?" Bert asked him.

Texaco shook his head. "My curiosity is at an all-time low," he replied. "I'll just tag along with you."

# Chapter Twenty-One

$T$HERE WAS STILL a trace of her perfume in the bedroom, a quiet floral scent. Dust was thick on the bureau, the desk, the open portable typewriter. Intricate spiderwebs festooned the desk lamp, the bedside lamp, and the bentwood frame of the wall mirror. The four-poster bed was still neatly made, its quilted spread faded and smeared with dust. The tan drapes were tight shut; nothing of the day outside got into Beverly Jepson's room.

"Gooseflesh," remarked Texaco when Bert clicked on the last of the lamps.

"Hum?"

"I'm suffering from a mild attack of goose bumps." He ran his hand up and down one arm. "This is like stepping back into the past."

"A nostalgic fellow like you ought to enjoy that."

"Hollywood in the forties is one thing, amigo, but stumbling around in a blooming shrine is something else again." Halting in the middle of the bedroom, Texaco took a slow look around. "They must've left this just about untouched since the day she walked into the ocean."

"Appears so." Bert seated himself at the desk and opened the top drawer.

After rubbing his hands together a few times, Texaco drifted over to the bureau. "Now I know how ghouls and grave robbers feel."

"Rejection slips, twenty years old and more, from the *Atlantic*, the *New Yorker*, and *Harper's*. But a personal P.S. on the *Harper's* one. 'Let's see more.' "

"A collector of vintage lingerie would enjoy my chore, but as for me . . . Olé! Maybe we've got us a photo of the mysterious gentleman friend." His probing fingers had touched a wooden picture-frame buried under the lacy slips.

Bert got up. "Is it?"

Texaco shook his head. "Might've been once. Ain't no more." He held up the empty frame. "I deduced, since she had this stashed away, that it might—"

"Her parents probably got rid of the picture but left the frame."

"Why?"

"Didn't like the guy, thought he was responsible for her death."

Texaco set the frame, face down, atop the bureau. Motes of dust danced up. "Or mayhap they wanted to avoid the bad breath of scandal. The bloke might've been married."

"Might've."

Texaco eased another drawer open and resumed his rummaging. "You alluded to Beverly Jepson's death. You think now she really is dead?"

"Her parents thought so."

"And you?"

Bert was going through a file folder of carbon copies of short stories. "I tend to think so, too."

"Then it isn't an older and wiser Beverly Jepson who's come back to seek revenge?" He shifted through bras and panties.

"Revenge is behind all this, but I can't see a slim woman like her being able to kill a hulk like Beau Jassminsky," answered Bert. "Or any of the others."

"Hell, in twenty long years the lady could've gained weight, studied Oriental martial arts, become a wrestler."

"Unlikely."

"Don't you know how good mystery yarns are constructed?" He commenced searching a new drawer. "Back a few years ago when Maximus was doing *Bloodthirsty Tales of Murder Comics* and *Foul Crimes Illustrated*, I made a detailed study of the classics of the mystery genre. Mainly so I'd have something to back me when I argued with Carlotsky about how rotten the scripts were," he explained. "In a first-class mystery you always look for the unlikely. You forget the guy with the obvious motive and opportunity and start musing about killer midgets who come down chimneys, tightrope walkers who can balance on the net of a tennis court, or snakes trained to climb five flights in a walk-up apartment building and zap the right victim."

"Would that life were so simple."

"My life sure is, simpler even than a typical Maximus comic-book plot. The Carrot family, for instance, leads a life of staggering variety compared to . . . What ho?"

Bert was on his hands and knees. He pulled the bottom desk drawer all the way out and free. "This one was sticking in an odd way."

"Something under there?"

After removing the papers and folders, Bert upended the drawer. A thick manila envelope was taped to the bottom. "Something," he replied.

Bert had the eleven letters spread out in two rows on their coffee table. Next to them were the doctor bills Jan had uncovered in the Jepson den. "I wish to hell he'd signed the letters," he said, frowning.

Texaco was sitting next to Jan on the sofa, eating a pita bread sandwich he'd constructed for himself in their kitchen. The day was just ending. "They're all nicely hand lettered," he said, "and lettering, to the trained eye of a hack artist, is as distinctive as handwriting or—"

"That's what's been bothering me about these letters."
Bert nodded twice. "I've seen this same style of printing
before."

His wife asked, "Where?"

"That's the trouble. I can't remember."

"It's pretty much," Texaco pointed out, "your standard
comic-book-style lettering."

"Wait a sec." Pivoting, Bert went trotting to his studio.

"You look glum, Mrs. K." Texaco took another deft bite
of his crowded sandwich, and only a few sprouts and bits
of lettuce fell from the pocket of bread down to the carpet.
"Feeling guilty about borrowing this stuff and bringing it
home?"

"No, I've been thinking about the Jepson girl." Absently,
Jan bent and gathered up the fallen scraps. "Having an
affair with a married man and then—"

"We'll check these out first." Bert had returned with a
slip of paper and a folded paper napkin. "This is the list
Mack Gruber obligingly printed for me, plus the one from
Marv Appel."

Texaco went over to watch as Bert compared the two
samples of lettering with that of the love letters they'd
found in Beverly Jepson's bedroom. "You can rule Gruber
out, amigo. Too many differences." He paused and chewed.
"His *S*'s, the *Y*'s, and those goofy *E*'s."

"Yep, Gruber's not the one," agreed Bert. "Don't think
Appel is either."

Perching on the coffee table edge, Texaco picked up the
nearest love letter. "The problem with Brer Appel is he's
much shakier these days."

"Yeah, but he makes his *B*'s, as quivery as they are,
differently than our letter writer. *S*'s, too. Fact is, he starts
the *S* at the top and this guy starts at the bottom."

Texaco dropped the letter. "No one's mentioned this
aloud, but maybe we're thinking it. So I might as well
state that Ty Banner didn't pen these tender missives either,"

he told them. "Although a brilliant artist, he can't letter for sour apples. Never could, and thus has to rely on capable young assistants such as myself."

"I've had notes from Ty, yeah, and you need a cryptographer to decipher them." Bert went over to sit beside Jan. "But damn, I know I've seen that exact same style of lettering. Recently."

"Up at Maximus maybe?" suggested Texaco.

"Nope."

"Jassminsky, Tunney, and Hibbard were all artists," Texaco said. "Did you see some of their—"

"That's not it either," said Bert. "Hell, I can't get it."

After chomping at his sandwich for a moment, Texaco said, "Look on the bright side. Our session of housebreaking netted quite a few new facts."

Rising, Bert began pacing. Twilight was growing outside the living-room windows.

Jan said, "We know Beverly Jepson was having an affair. The man was married but promised to leave his wife soon and marry Beverly. He was, judging by the hints he drops, a few years older than her."

"Was he sincere, though?" asked Texaco. "Or just leading her astray?"

"I think he was really trying to get out of what he thought was a bad marriage," answered Jan. "But he sounds like the sort of man who couldn't simply confront his wife and ask for a divorce."

"We also know," added Bert, "that he was someone who saw her regularly. Not just on their occasional secret dates, but in some other normal context. School, work, socially."

Texaco settled into an armchair and finished the last bite of his pita sandwich. "Suppose this phantom lover was employed at Kreative Komics?"

Bert shook his head. "The dates don't match for that, far as I can tell," he said. "This guy was writing her before she left college. And in this fourth letter, he seems to be talking about not seeing her as much now because of the new job in New York City."

"Too bad she didn't save the envelopes," said Jan. "That'd give us a postmark town."

"He was obviously local," said Bert. "He talks about meeting her various places in Westport, Weston, even New Haven once."

"Ah, but consider this," put in Texaco, pointing ceiling-ward with his right forefinger. "This lad knew that decades later, someone would peruse these letters, and he slipped in false facts to throw us off."

"Sounds like something Carlotsky would plot for *Foul Crimes Illustrated*," said Bert.

"The saddest part," said Jan, "is that she might have been pregnant when she killed herself."

Bert tapped the letters and then the pile of doctor's bills. "He mentions that possibility twice in these letters, the final two," he said. "But he doesn't seem to be sure. These doctor's bills seem to indicate she started seeing the family physician with increasing regularity about two months or so before she died. Before that she hadn't been in for a year. Unfortunately I can't make out these scribbles, so we don't know if he really was testing her for pregnancy and then treating her."

"This means that the mystery swain is the proud father," said Texaco, "not one of the guys who raped her?"

"The dates are wrong for that," said Jan. "If she was seeing the doctor because she thought she was pregnant, then it started before she was raped."

Texaco gave a deep sigh. "Ty is right. Many of us lead soap opera lives."

Bert picked up the final letter. " 'I don't understand what's going on, Beverly. You haven't showed up at any of our usual arranged meeting places, you haven't even written to me or telephoned. Whenever I could, I came by and parked near your house. You don't even seem to come out. If you are pregnant, then that's something to be happy about. We can, as I've been telling you, work it out. Please get in touch with me, Beverly. If I don't hear from you soon, I intend to break our standing rule. I'll phone you at home, and if that doesn't work, I shall come to the house. Perhaps it's time your parents . . .' "

Jan said, "Sounds as though she never got in touch with him after she was raped."

"He sure doesn't mention it in the letters," said Bert. "Going by the date on this one and of the KK party, she seems not to have communicated with him after the attack. Simply quit her job, came home, put her affairs in order, and . . . killed herself."

"She should've told him," said Jan. "It might've helped."

"That's a rough thing to talk about," said her husband. "Being raped by five guys."

"Aw, he wasn't up to comforting her anyway," said Texaco, sitting up in his chair. "To me he sounds like a weak, indecisive type. I mean, hell, if you hadn't heard from your love in a week or two . . . do you write her a letter? He lived in the vicinity. Go to her damn house, barge right in. That's the way to handle it."

"He had a wife," said Bert. "And maybe a position that would be jeopardized if there was trouble. A lot of these big firms in Fairfield County frown on adultery among their executives. Especially twenty years ago."

"Love knows no boundaries," said Texaco. "Me, I'd have climbed her balcony and carried her off."

"I don't agree with you about him, Juan," she said. "Sure, there's a stiffness in some of his phrasing, an uneasiness. But I'll bet you anything the guy really loved her. That much really comes across. If she'd told him what had happened, he wouldn't have turned his back on her."

"She was a pretty sensitive young woman," said Bert. "I skimmed through some of her short stories, and . . . well, it seems to me this might have been her first big romance.

An affair, then the attack—it was just too much guilt for her to handle."

"Remind me to leave a fully notarized suicide note," remarked Texaco. "Thus avoiding this sort of postmortem speculation about my motives and my innermost secrets."

Bert said to him, "I'm damn near sure she's the reason for these killings, Texaco. That's why I'm spending so much time going over this stuff."

The little cartoonist said, "Have you ruled out the possibility it's Mack Gruber, hell-bent for revenge?"

Bert gestured at the letters. "The guy that wrote these is probably the killer. That's what I feel."

"Then as soon as you recall where you laid eyes on that lettering before," said Texaco, "you'll have him."

"If," said Bert, "I can remember."

# Chapter Twenty-Two

*B*ERT DIDN'T REMEMBER until the next afternoon.

He'd gone into New York to have lunch with the art director of Apex Books. It had been a successful lunch, and he'd come away with an assignment to do covers for the paperback reprints of two suspense best-sellers.

Bert was trying to skim the hardcover edition of one of them, *The Quackenbush Confrontation*, as the 3:05 Metro-North commuter train carried him from Manhattan to the Westport station.

The plot was a complex one, and the story took place in Amsterdam, various cities in Ethiopia, Paris, and other locales. He doodled notions for his cover painting in his notebook, but his mind kept going elsewhere.

Shutting the first book, he attempted to read the other. This was entitled *The Wagenheim Reversal*, and the opening chapter took place at the University of Heidelberg in 1933. As the train rushed across the spring afternoon, passing through slums and quaint villages, his thoughts kept returning to the unsigned love letters.

Where the hell did I see that same lettering? he asked himself.

They passed over a small river. He glanced out at the marina below with its sailboats and launches. He still didn't know the name of this particular river.

Back to the University of . . .

Bert stiffened, sat up, closed the novel. "Warren Snyder."

The balding man in the seat ahead of him looked back. "Beg pardon?"

"Sorry, thinking out loud."

"You in advertising?"

"Not exactly."

"Ad men do a lot of mumbling." He returned to his *USA Today.*

Bert had remembered where he'd seen that lettering before. At the University of Brimstone, a week ago, when he'd dropped in on Professor Snyder's classroom.

Sure, he'd been writing names on the damn blackboard. Printing them in the same style.

Maybe handwriting experts couldn't swear to something like that. Bert remembered reading someplace that block lettering was next to impossible to pin down. But any cartoonist, as Texaco had mentioned, could recognize an individual letterer.

So it was Warren Snyder who had written the love letters to Beverly Jepson. He was the married man she had her affair with, and probably the father of her unborn child. He'd met her while she was a student at UB and he was a teacher. Another reason for keeping their romance quiet.

Snyder really had loved her. Now he was killing the men who'd raped her and triggered her suicide.

But why the hell did he wait twenty long years? Maybe it took the guy that long to get goofy enough to . . .

No, it was because he didn't know before.

He had never seen Beverly after the attack, never even talked to her on the phone. He never knew she'd been raped.

All these years he never knew the reason for her killing herself. Hell, he probably blamed himself. Thought she didn't want to have the child.

Twenty years of never being sure.

Then one night he's sitting at the rap session and Fred Hibbard calmly starts talking about Beverly Jepson. Tells how he and his buddies drugged her and gang raped her. Got away with it, too, because she was afraid, ashamed. She never talked about it. Instead she walked into the Sound. Of course, they hadn't expected her to do anything that drastic. Made them all feel guilty as hell afterwards. But, you know, you get drunk and horny. It wasn't exactly like they beat her up or hurt her that way. They just made love to her. Christ, a lot of girls would just relax and enjoy it, like the proverb says. Except Bev was sort of strange, too damn sensitive for her own good. Sure, he still felt really bad about that. That's why he was bringing it up after all this time. It's a very rough thing to live with.

Snyder sat there and listened. Pretended sympathy for Hibbard, joined into the discussion later, offered tips and helpful suggestions on how to cope with guilt feelings.

Inside, though, he was making up his mind to pay them back. Every damn one who'd touched her. They'd murdered Beverly Jepson as far as Snyder was concerned. Murdered her and got away with it. And here was Hibbard almost bragging about it. Well, now they'd pay. One by one.

So Snyder sits there, looking interested and probably even makes a few notes to help him keep track of the helpful points he's going to make. Actually he wrote down the names Hibbard gave out.

Leon Brenner.

Beau Jassminsky.

Marvin Appel.

Fred Hibbard.

Dolph Tunney.

Ty Banner.

"Jesus, he must have Ty's name on his goddamn list. Because . . . Sorry, mumbling again."

The balding man gave him an understanding smile before turning around.

Fred Hibbard's memory was a bit shaky, and in his past accounts of the rape he'd included Ty's name. Chances were he did that at the rap session, too. Sure, Ty had a feeling something negative had been said against him that night he wasn't there.

That meant Ty and Marv Appel were both in danger.

The overhead speakers squawked, "Norwalk–South Norwalk coming up. Norwalk–South Norwalk."

Maybe I ought to get off one station ahead of my stop, phone Detective Furtado and Ty.

No, his car was parked in the Westport lot. Be better to get that, in case he had to drive over to Ty's or to see the policeman.

Don't panic, he advised himself.

The train slowed and stopped at the Norwalk station. The man in front of him grabbed his attaché case off the overhead rack and started down the aisle. "Don't let 'em get you down," he called as he hurried for the doors.

Nodding absently, Bert returned to thinking about Warren Snyder.

Could he prove any of this?

Furtado might not be convinced by the lettering business. Texaco would understand that, so would Ty. Probably a cop wouldn't.

Wait a minute. There was something else he knew about Professor Snyder, something that tied in.

The doors hissed shut, the train started rolling again.

Something about an alibi for Snyder? Yeah, about one of the murders.

Dolph Tunney was killed on a Monday night, remembered Bert, disappointed. The rap sessions are on Mondays at eight, so Professor Snyder couldn't have killed him. Yep, I know he was there that night. Because Ty told me how he'd come in a few minutes late because he'd been waterbagged while crossing campus and didn't have time to . . .

Hey!

The killer had held Dolph Tunney under the water in his bathtub. Struggled with him, kept his head down until he drowned.

You'd maybe get a little wet doing that.

Okay, Snyder did it and got himself wet. Coat sleeves splashed, pants spotted. But he can't go change, because he has to be at the session. Sure, they can't pinpoint the death. So if respectable Professor Snyder says he was at the rap session at about the time Tunney drowned, he ought to be able to get away with it. But what he really did was stop by Tunney's, kill him in a few minutes, and then speed over to the session. Everything went fine, except for the wet clothes. And he explained that away.

Besides, the police wrote Tunney's death off as an accident. And if anyone got suspicious about Snyder's activities that night, they'd never come up with a motive for his killing Tunney.

Soon as I hit Westport, I'll phone Detective Furtado. And Ty.

He had to warn Ty about Snyder, then explain to Furtado what he'd found out. If they went up against the professor with the letters and the rest of it, he might admit—

The train made a sudden and unexpected stop.

After flickering for a few seconds, all the lights in the car went out. The air-conditioning died.

"Good old dependable Metro-North," sighed a plump lady across the aisle.

The train sat.

Bert checked his wristwatch. 4:16 already. They should've arrived in Westport, which was only a few minutes up the damn track, around 4:05.

The train sat.

Christ, I have to get to a phone.

A gray-haired executive a few seats up ahead said to his

younger executive seatmate, "Remember last month? We sat here for three bloody hours."

"One time last winter we were stranded just outside Stamford for seven. My wife and I were having a cocktail party that same night and I came schlepping home about . . ."

Bert rubbed his thumb across his fingertips. Snyder might be on his way to Ty or Appel right now.

"Ladies and gentlemen," rasped the speakers, "we have a slight mechanical problem. We'll be fixing it very soon. Thank you for your patience."

"Slight mechanical problem?" said the fat lady. "The engine probably fell off the tracks."

"They said 'slight mechanical problem' last month and then we sat on our duffs until nightfall."

Looking around the car, Bert spotted no sign of a conductor. Wouldn't do him much good if he did find one. They never let you off one of these damn stalled trains. The doors remained steadfastly shut and you waited.

But I have to warn Ty.

The train sat.

# Chapter Twenty-Three

$E$LLEN BANNER OPENED the door. "Bert, is there something wrong?" she asked. "You look somewhat distraught."

"Is Ty here?"

"No, he—"

"Tried to call you from the train station, but all the damn phones on the platform were tied up," he said, a faint wheeze sounding in his chest. "The 3:05 didn't get into Westport until 5:17."

"That's far from being the record for lateness." The blonde woman opened the door wider. "Want to come in and catch your breath?"

"Ran to my car," he explained, entering the big house. "Easier to drive over here than wait for the phones to be free."

"You still haven't expl—"

"Listen, where exactly is Ty?"

"He's off on one of his self-improving hikes."

"Alone?"

"Alone, yes." A frown was on her face. "What is the—"

"Where'd he go?"

"He decided to drive over to Devil's Den, that nature preserve in Weston. Ty likes to hike through there about once every couple of—"

"How long ago did he leave here?"

"About four. It takes something like twenty minutes to

drive there," she replied, frown deepening. "Bert, what is all this about?"

"Nothing maybe. I don't know. I'm not sure."

"Does it have something to do with these deaths?"

"No." He looked away from her blue eyes. "Yes, probably."

"You think something's going to happen to Ty?" She touched his arm.

"Does anyone else know he's going to be there?"

"No, Ty just up and decided to go . . . well, yes, a couple people do know. But I—"

"Who?"

"He had two phone calls after he left. I did mention where he was. Still, that—"

"Who phoned?"

"Bud Heinz, to complain about his new *Seaweed Sam* contract," she answered. "Then one of the fellows from his rap group. Professor Snyder."

"Snyder," Bert said quietly.

"He just wanted to ask Ty about their—"

"Can I use your phone, Ellen?"

"What's going on?"

"Could be nothing. The thing is—"

"There's a phone on the end table." She pointed toward the living room.

Hurrying over to the phone, Bert punched out his own number.

"Bert?" Jan answered with.

"Me. The damn train was late."

"You okay?"

"Sure, fine. But I don't think I'll be home for a few hours."

"Where are you?"

"Right now I'm at Ty's, but I'll be heading—"

"Is he all right? You sound very distraught."

"People keep telling me that," he said to his wife. "Far

156

as I know Ty's fine. Don't worry. See you soon as I can."

"You aren't planning to—"

He hung up. Next he called information for the numbers of the University of Brimstone and Warren Snyder's home. The professor couldn't be located on campus and no one answered his home phone.

After that Bert put through a call to Detective Furtado.


The real name of Devil's Den was the Lucius Pond Ordway Preserve. It was located in the town of Weston, roughly ten miles inland from Westport, and consisted of several dozen acres of woods, trails, marshes, ledges, and streams. Although Bert had wandered through the unspoiled acres a few times, he didn't feel he was an expert at finding his way around.

He parked his car in the small lot off the Godfrey Road entrance. There were only five other cars and one of them was Ty Banner's six-year-old gray Porsche.

Bert checked the other cars, but found nothing to indicate one of them belonged to Warren Snyder.

He wouldn't leave his car here anyway probably.

There was an open registration book on a rough-hewn podium. Ty's name, signed the way he signed it on his comic strip, was there with the time he'd arrived. 4:47. Over an hour ago.

There was no way of telling which way Ty had gone, or how much ground he'd covered. Bert decided to try the nearest pathway. This one went climbing gradually through low, rocky hills and a wooded area.

Damn, why didn't I pay more attention that year I was in the Cub Scouts? Then I might be able to pick up his trail.

After Bert climbed for nearly ten minutes he heard voices. Picking up his pace as best he could, he hurried upward toward the crest of the hill.

*157*

Two twelve-year-old boys and a black-and-tan mutt were coming up toward him.

"What time is it, sir?" asked the smaller one, a freckled kid in camouflage pants, sweatshirt and painter's cap.

"Ten past six."

"I told you, John," the boy said to his companion.

"You sure it isn't 5:30?" John asked him.

"Wish it was," answered Bert. "Listen, I'm looking for a friend of—"

The dog had been sniffing closer and now decided to start barking at him.

"Scrappy!" ordered John. "Quit that."

The dog persisted, head low and glaring up at Bert.

"Easy, boy," suggested Bert. "About my friend. He's a tall man, graying hair. Probably wearing a golf sweater."

John caught Scrappy by the collar. "Stop it, Scrap."

The other boy asked, "An old man?"

"I guess so, by your standards."

"An artist or something? He had a sketchbook," said the boy, pointing over his shoulder. "We saw him . . . when was it, John?"

John was still struggling with the dog, who seemed anxious to take a nip at Bert. "Half hour ago."

"Where?"

"We were coming back along the trail from Singer Pond."

"Which path is that?" He had to shout to be heard above the barking and complaining of Scrappy.

"Downhill and go left."

"Right," corrected John.

"Left."

John grabbed up the dog, hugged it to him. He gave an exasperated shake of his head. "Right, dummy."

The other boy turned, adjusted his cap, gazed back the way they'd come. "Oh, yeah. It's the one to the right."

"Dumb," said his friend. "We got to go."

"Thanks for your help." Skirting the boy and the dog, Bert started down.

Bert saw Banner first, a hundred yards down the trail. He was sitting on a fallen log beside a wide pond, his sketchbook open across his knees.

Fringing the small clearing were maple and birch trees. That's where Bert spotted Warren Snyder.

The professor, wearing dark slacks, a dark pullover, and a ski mask, was crouched in among the trees fifty feet to the right of Banner. Clutched in his black-gloved hand was a jagged rock. Snyder seemed about ready to charge at Ty.

Before he did that, though, he took a look around to be sure no one was nearby.

He saw Bert then, and their eyes locked for what felt like a long time.

Snyder broke contact first, spun, began running.

"Ty!" shouted Bert. "Look out."

But the professor was running away from the cartoonist, not toward him.

Banner, mouth dropping open, jumped up. His sketchbook tumbled to the mossy ground. "What the hell, my boy?"

"Snyder, he's the killer," Bert yelled in a gasping voice as he dived into the woods.

He stumbled, cracked his shoulder against a tree trunk, kept on.

The retreating professor wasn't having a smooth time of it either. He tripped over a dead branch and went sprawling into a clump of brush. He struggled to his feet, staggering, and then continued on.

Bert took advantage of that stumble to shorten the distance between them. "Snyder," he called out, "it's all over. Quit."

Professor Snyder kept on for another hundred feet. He

halted then. Shrugging, he turned to face Bert. "Yes, you're right."

Bert slowed, approaching him carefully. "I'd feel better if you'd drop that rock."

After looking at the stone in his hand as though it were someone else's that he'd picked up by mistake, Snyder let it fall to the ground. "I almost got them all," he said, voice muffled by the mask.

"Ty wasn't one of them."

"Yes, he was. Hibbard knew and he—"

"His memory was a mite fuzzy by the time he got around to recounting the story at your rap session."

"That it was," seconded Banner, who'd just caught up with them and was brushing bits of twig off the sleeve of his golf sweater.

While he tugged off the wool ski mask, Snyder said, "You'd deny it now to—"

"C'mon, Warren," said Banner. "I wouldn't lie at a time like this. I never had a damn thing to do with the rape. Even you ought to know me better than that. I always marry the women I want to sleep with."

The professor said, "I was right about the others."

"Yep," said Bert, "they were all involved. Five of them."

Nodding, Snyder said, "All these years I believed she killed herself because she didn't want my child. I really was intending to get a divorce. There were complications, but Beverly and I could have been married. In fact, I did get a divorce anyway, a few months after she died." He looked from Bert to Ty. "Everything would've worked out fine . . . she was a marvelous girl . . . You knew her, Ty."

Ty said quietly, "Sure, she was special."

"She was . . . she was such a marvelous person . . . I . . . You know, you marry young and then . . . then you meet the woman you should have married." He rubbed his gloved hands together, twisting the ski mask up into a ball. "I was planning this . . . working toward the divorce,

160

and . . . then I lost Beverly and my child. . . . She . . . after what they did . . . she wouldn't even talk to me or tell me what had happened. I thought . . . what anyone would've thought, obviously . . . I felt she didn't love me anymore. . . . Then she killed herself. I assumed . . . that it was because of me. . . . You know, I still see her walking into the water . . . I dream of that at least once a week. Twenty years I've carried that around, the guilt and shame."

"You might have," said Bert, "broken your rule about never going to her house. You could've confronted her and—"

"No, that wouldn't have worked. Her parents were . . . very conservative people."

"Even so, if—"

"My boy, it's all over and done," reminded Banner. "Nobody can mend the past. Not by saying 'I should've done this' and not by killing bastards like Beau Jassminsky and Fred Hibbard."

"I never knew what had happened," said Snyder, hands clutching the black mask. "Then a few weeks ago, in that stupid rap session, Hibbard opens up and talks about the rape. They, none of them, ever knew I was involved with Beverly. No one did, not even her parents. That was so terrible when she was gone . . . I couldn't talk about it to anyone."

"Must've been rough sitting there and listening to that," said Banner.

"Yes, and I had to act as though it was just another story. I listened to Hibbard recount it, the terrible thing they'd done to her. He claimed to feel very upset and guilty, even now, yet you could sense a touch of pride in his voice." Snyder nodded to himself. "When he mentioned the names of all of them, I knew what I had to do. What I'd been waiting to do, actually. I had to kill them all, every one of them who took her from me . . . her and my unborn son."

"You killed Leon Brenner, too?" Bert asked.

The day was beginning to fade; light was slowly leaving the woods.

"He was the first," answered the professor. "I found out where he lived, watched his home." He smiled, mostly to himself. "That was the easiest one, since Brenner was a dying man anyway. I smothered him with his own pillow. He was awake when I came into his room, but very weak. When he tried to sit up I simply told him, 'This is because of Beverly Jepson.' Then I killed him. I actually don't know if he understood me, since he was heavily sedated."

"Each one had to look like an accident," said Bert.

"Of course," said Professor Snyder. "My revenge was a private thing, and I certainly didn't want to get caught before I'd taken care of them all."

"When you killed Beau Jassminsky he was still in his house, wasn't he?"

"Yes, getting ready to go out and run," said Snyder. "I stopped by his house when I knew he was alone, pretending my car had broken down and asking to use his phone." He laughed. "He refused to let me, by the way. Told me there was a gas station a mile down the road. I knocked him out, put the rest of his gear on him and dumped him. Making sure afterwards everything pointed to an accident. I take it I made a mistake there somewhere?"

"Wrong kind of shoes," said Bert.

The professor's left shoulder rose. "Well, I'm not a runner," he said. "Although I ought to have caught that touch, since I did study each of them before I made my move."

"And you murdered Dolph Tunney on the way to your rap session?" said Bert. "That's how you got wet."

"He struggled more than I'd counted on, yes," replied Snyder. "I hadn't time to change, and hadn't thought to bring dry clothes in my car. But I had to be at the session near eight, in case I needed an alibi. Although I didn't, as it turned out. Not until you began nosing around, Kurrie."

162

Banner said, "Might I suggest we escort the professor to the nearest police station?"

"I'll cooperate," said Snyder. "No use struggling now." He turned toward Bert. "So Marv Appel was the only one I failed on?"

"He's the last one left," said Bert, taking hold of the professor's arm.

Snyder stuffed the ski mask down into his trouser pocket. He took a brief look around at the darkening woodland. "He'd be a grown man now, you know, almost through college."

Bert asked, "Who?"

"My son, the one who died with her in the Sound."

# Chapter Twenty-Four

$B$ERT RAN AN extra mile on Saturday morning and he didn't wheeze any more than usual. When he returned to the kitchen, he had a look of accomplishment on his perspiring face.

Jan was brewing herself a pot of peppermint tea. "Ah, fame," she sighed.

"Eh?"

"You had three phone calls already and it's barely 10:00 A.M."

"Business on Saturday?"

His wife shook her head. "This is still the murder case," she told him. "Channel Eight in New Haven wants to send out a crew to interview you for a segment on a show called, I think, *Newsworthy*."

He brushed at his hair, nodding. "Another Amateur Sleuth Nabs Mass Murderer sort of thing?"

"What else? They didn't sound like they wanted to talk about your art career."

"Still, you know," he said as he seated himself at the kitchen table, "if they come here to interview me in my studio I can casually have some of my finished covers lined up in the background."

"Heck, you might as well display the things in the foreground."

"Who else called?"

"A fellow claiming to be a reporter from *News* magazine."

"*News?* Hey, that's the biggest one so far. Maybe we'll get *Time* next."

"Vanity, vanity," she warned. "The third call was . . . brace yourself . . . Carlotsky."

"What the hell did he want?"

"He's trying to woo you back to Maximus Comics." She consulted a memo she'd written to herself. "He sounded, for him, close to cordial. Anyway, if I have the details right, Maximus is eager to have you do a miniseries of direct-sale graphic novels for something called *Mystery Tales Illustrated*. Does that sound right so far? Carlotsky was anxious to know if you'd be interested in drawing, and maybe scripting as well, the first three. Twelve thousand dollars per each forty-eight-page book. He mentioned that they wanted to put a . . . 'tasteful' was his exact word . . . a tasteful banner across each cover. *Drawn By A Real Life Private Eye! Only Maximus Has Him!* Tasteful."

"I'll pass on that one."

"Thirty-six thousand dollars for three comic books doesn't tempt you?"

Bert considered. "The money tempts me, yes," he admitted. "But then I think of working for Carlotsky and Maximus again, and that pretty well kills the temptation. When's *News* coming out to see me?"

"He'll call again." She poured herself a cup of tea. "Want some?"

"Orange juice after a run is my motto." Getting up, he went to the refrigerator. "Boy, fourteen newspapers, nine radio shows, a news service, six TV channels in Connecticut and New York, and now *News*. Not bad."

"What's the protocol for this sort of thing?" Jan asked as she stirred a spoonful of honey into her tea. "Just because you caught a killer, does that mean we have to withdraw from society or go into a period of mourning or anything?"

"What are you contemplating?"

"Well, we've all been through stress and strain of late," she said, "on top of which we've just moved into a new house and are finally all unpacked. Could we throw ourselves a housewarming, say, two weeks from today?"

After pouring himself a glass of juice, he answered, "Sure. Large party or small?"

"Couple dozen friends."

"Do we have that many friends?"

"By adding a couple of ringers and my dad, we can just about make twenty-four, yes."

Bert sat once more. "What would you think about asking Furtado and his wife?"

"The policeman?"

"That Furtado, yes. We're not exactly buddies, but he wound up treating me pretty well."

"And well he should, since you solved a series of murders in Brimstone and environs."

"He got the Weston police to send an officer over to Devil's Den when we grabbed Snyder," he said. "Also had the Bridgeport cops keep an eye on Appel in case the professor made a try for him that day. And we've had a couple of long chats since."

"Suppose I put him tentatively on the guest list," she suggested, "and you see how you feel when we send out the invitations next week?"

"Okay," Bert said. "Maybe it's not a good notion to socialize with the law."

"I did put Carolyn Frame on the list, assuming she—"

"Nope, you can scratch her."

"Aren't you and she still—"

"More or less, but Carolyn won't be in town," he explained. "She's taking some time off, going to California for a few weeks. She might even look for a newspaper job out there."

"She was really in love with Dolph Tunney, huh?"

"She was, and being around here depresses her."

"From what I've heard, he wasn't a very admirable man."

"Every woman doesn't have your discrimination and taste."

"Funny," said Jan, "it was Carolyn who really got you into all this. But she's in worse shape now than—"

"I was too late to save Tunney, remember."

"How the heck could you have saved his life? That night you were going to visit him you had no idea what was—"

"Yeah, but maybe I could've pushed Furtado harder about Beau Jassminsky's death, got him digging into this earlier."

"You saved Ty's life, Marv Appel's, too. That's the important thing."

"I know, but still . . ." He tapped his fingers on the table top. "This whole mess hasn't been as clear-cut as I'd have liked, Jan. The guys I was trying to save were rapists, except for Ty. They drove a girl to suicide, ruined Snyder's life and—"

"Wait now," his wife cut in. "It usually takes more than an attack to drive a person to suicide. When you kill yourself, it's the end of your whole life. You don't, even now, know what Beverly Jepson was like, what her parents were like. Her suicide might have been building for years."

"I also have mixed feelings about Professor Snyder. He's supposed to be a damn good teacher, a—"

"Sure, and every time some madman guns down a dozen of his neighbors with a shotgun, the survivors say, 'Why, he was such a nice, quiet boy. And, my, so bright.'" She shook her head. "Bert, Snyder murdered four people. He was intending to kill Ty. Damn it, he might even have tried for you."

168

"I know, I know."

"And nobody forced Snyder to brood and mourn for over twenty years. For some reason, he got stuck back there in the past, and killing these men seemed like a way out. But he was crazy."

"Guess maybe I wasn't cut out to be KnightOwl or Captain Thunderbolt. Sometimes it's tough to tell the good guys from the bad guys."

She sipped her tea. "Texaco," she said.

"In what context?"

"Will he have a date for our party or should I play matchmaker and invite a single young lady who looks like a vanished starlet?"

"I'd better check with him and let you know." He eyed her. "Would you actually loose him on someone you know?"

"He's very sweet and charming."

"Texaco?"

"He's sort of cute, too."

"Texaco?"

"Your artist's eye ought to tell you that," she said. "Oh, and I'm inviting Tess Anderson and the fellow she's living with at the moment."

"How's that modeling for her Boutiques, Inc. stores going?"

"We have our first photo session on Tuesday."

"Good. Your being a model again'll make me the envy of my peers."

"I've seen most of their wives, and outshining them isn't much of an accomplishment."

"Vanity, vanity." He pushed back from the table. "I think I'll take a little drive."

"Where to?"

"Oh, over to Westport. Down to the beach."

"Want me to come along?"

"Actually I just want to take a walk along the Sound by myself for awhile."

"Do you know the actual spot?"

"What spot?" he asked, leaving his chair.

"Where Beverly Jepson walked into the sea."

"No, nobody ever told me the exact location and I never got around to looking it up." He walked to the door. "I'll be back in an hour or so."

"Take as long as you need," she said.